W9-AXI-012

The Man Everybody Was Afraid Of

A RINEHART SUSPENSE NOVEL

OTHER DAVE BRANDSTETTER MYSTERIES
BY JOSEPH HANSEN

Troublemaker
Death Claims
Fadeout

A RINEHART SUSPENSE NOVEL

JOSEPH HANSEN

The Man Everybody Was Afraid Of

HOLT, RINEHART AND WINSTON

New York

Copyright © 1978 by Joseph Hansen
All rights reserved, including the right to reproduce
this book or portions thereof in any form.
Published simultaneously in Canada by Holt, Rinehart
and Winston of Canada, Limited.

Library of Congress Cataloging in Publication Data
Hansen, Joseph, 1923–
The man everybody was afraid of.
(A Rinehart suspense novel)
I. Title.
PZ4.H247Man [PS3558.A513] 813'.5'4 78-4190
ISBN 0-03-042376-7

Designer: Amy Hill
Printed in the United States of America
10 9 8 7 6 5 4 3 2 1

For George and Patti Hodgkin
and their genius loci

The Man Everybody Was Afraid Of

A RINEHART SUSPENSE NOVEL

1

In 1964 a tidal wave knocked down the shacks next to the abandoned fish cannery at La Caleta, and the wreckage the Pacific didn't take, bulldozers did. The cannery itself was strong and it remained as built, one end on the beach, the rest over the water, its paint scaling under a rusty corrugated-iron roof. Boards had dropped out of its side decks but the pilings were upright and still supported a winch crusty with old salt. A chainlink fence topped by sagging barbwire enclosed the cannery grounds. NO TRESPASSING signs hung off the fence. Double gates fastened with a shiny chain and padlock cut off the road down to the loading bays. Weeds had broken the blacktop, and sand had half smothered it.

Dave could remember when the place functioned. Back before the war, back when he was a kid. Mexican people lived in the vanished shacks and worked in the cannery. You could see it from the highway. On trips north, ignoring the complaints of this or that young stepmother, he used to make his father stop the Marmon, the Auburn, the Lincoln Zephyr, so he could stand at the road edge and watch the wide, wallowing boats unload their cargo, slippery silver in the sun. There would be strong stinks of raw fish, of fish cooking, the rumble of the canning machines above the roar of surf, the wind-torn shouts of fishermen and dockers. It was a long time ago.

He was middle aged now. His father was an old man, maybe as old as he was going to get. He lay this morning on a high bed in a gray room whose coral-color door was marked INTENSIVE CARE. A triangle of foggy plastic masked his nose and mouth. Thin tubing snaked from the mask to an oxygen tank. Frail wires were taped to the bruised backs of his hands. They fed into metal boxes at the head of the bed. One of the boxes had a blue disk across which a shaky line of lavender scribbled news of his torn heart. On the other box an orange light winked, winked, stammered, winked out, winked on again.

All night, leaning on the foot of the bed, Dave had watched the lights, while girls in starchy white moved in and out of shadow, making notes, counting the sick pulse. Twice they had put Dave out in the hall to sit on a chair of coral-color molded plastic and read his watch and smoke his mouth dry. When he'd gone back in, nothing had changed. Once, his father's head had lain against the bed's guard bars. He'd straightened it on the alien pillows.

At six-thirty this morning, when Amanda appeared—in jeans and boots, turtleneck jersey, Navajo necklace, cowhide shirt-jacket—Dave left. If his father woke, he'd be as happy to see his new young wife as his aging homosexual son. Maybe happier. If he didn't wake, he'd never know the

2

difference. There was nothing Dave could do. And he hated the helplessness. He went to work.

The road he now drove skirted the cannery fence, cut into a bluff, climbed from the beach and curved off, so that the cannery went out of sight. The road was private. It led to a 1920s Spanish colonial house of white stucco with red tile roofs. The house stood alone among trees and looked down at a quiet cove of the rocky little bay that gave La Caleta its simpleminded name. The house had been built by the cannery owner. After the war finished off his business, it had stood empty for years. Ben Orton had bought it in the early fifties, lived in it, raised a son and daughter in it, died in it. By violence, of course. Orton was a rough man.

Dave left the car by the road under a big oleander drunk with pink blossom. Gravel crunched beneath his shoes as he climbed a curved driveway edged by whitewashed rocks and flowering ivy geranium. A double garage made a wing of the house. One of its doors was up. A pale lavender Montego waited inside. Sun glared off the house windows. They were set in wide arches and the curtains were drawn. Deep in a smaller arch he found a door with rough black iron hardware. He used the knocker. Hollowness echoed beyond it but he knew she was home. He'd telephoned ten minutes ago just to hear her say hello.

He stepped out of the doorway shadow to look between the slim trunks of lacy eucalyptus trees to the bay below. It was an assortment of blues. Tangled rafts of brown kelp floated there. Sea otters lived among these. He looked for the bob of a sleek head or for a gull darting low over the surface. Otters were sloppy feeders; a gull or two always hung around for scraps. He'd need binoculars to be sure but he doubted there were otters today. The gulls soared high and lazy in the warm blue air. He heard heel taps, the rattle of a latch, and he turned to the open door.

She was plump, blond, forty-five, with dark patches under her eyes that said she'd been sleeping badly. Television crews had filmed Orton's funeral. Clips had made the six o'clock news even 250 miles down the coast in Los Angeles. Uniforms, flags, gun salute. Orton had once been a Marine. On the nineteen-inch diagonal screen his widow had worn this dress, black, simple, set off by a single strand of pearls. Her hair had looked newly set. It still did. Her lipstick was muted pink and matched the enamel on her nails, except she'd been picking at the enamel, chipping it. Her eyes were round and blue and they widened at him.

He said, "Mrs. Orton? Brandstetter—Medallion Life." He handed her a card that she didn't look at. She kept the little girl eyes on him. They looked wary. He explained, "Your husband's life was insured with us."

She said bitterly, "That didn't save it." Her voice was childlike too, and the words it had spoken seemed to shock her. "Excuse me. I'm not myself." She drew breath, turned up the corners of a sweet mouth. "What may I do for you?"

"In cases where a policyholder's death is not from natural causes, we make an investigation."

"Investigation." Her laugh said she thought he was joking. "My husband was chief of police here. There's been a thorough investigation."

"I read the police reports," Dave said, "this morning."

"And the arrest report? The man who killed Ben is locked up, Mr.—" she glanced at the card, "Brandstetter. The case is closed."

"It looks that way," Dave said. "But I have to follow routine." He gave her a half smile. "A policeman's wife

4

must be familiar with that word. I can't copy reports. I have to do my own digging and come up with my own answers."

"But it seems such a waste of time." She folded the card, making the crease sharp with her nails. "What can one man expect to find that a whole police force couldn't?"

"Probably nothing." He shrugged amiably. "That's the usual outcome of routine, isn't it?" He coaxed her with another smile and took a step forward. "I'll try not to take up much of your time."

"Oh, time." Her mouth twisted bleakly. "What have I got but time?" But she didn't retreat and ask him in. She tilted her head and frowned. "Your accounting people need a report from you before they can send a check, is that it?"

"That's it." He smiled one more time.

She didn't return the smile. "Mr. Brandstetter—Ben Orton was killed by a blow that shattered his skull. That couldn't have been suicide."

He didn't tell her that other things besides suicide could get in the way of payment on a policy. He said, "I've been checking out death claims for twenty years, Mrs. Orton. The investigation of your husband's murder not only wasn't thorough—it hardly happened."

"That can't be true." She folded the card back on itself. Her knuckles were white. "Those men thought the world of Ben. They'd have done anything to catch his killer."

"They didn't even try," Dave said gently. "They settled for the obvious."

"Cliff Kerlee. Well, why not? His bag—what do you call them?—that big dirty pouch thing with the leather fringes —it was lying there, right by Ben's body."

"Kerlee claims he wasn't here—not then, not ever."

"What would you expect him to say?" Her laugh was

5

scornful. "He'd shouted at the top of his voice that he wanted to kill Ben. On television. Everybody heard him."

"It's a common expression, Mrs. Orton. Ugly, but not often literal. I doubt that it was the first time anyone said it about your husband. He was a controversial man. He had enemies."

"Radicals, dope addicts, degenerates." She thrust out a soft little chin. "He didn't care what they said. He stood for what made this country great."

The sun was heating up. It made Dave sleepy. He told her, "In the police report, Hector Rodriguez, who works for Kerlee and lives with him, says the man didn't leave his place on Sunday."

"What else would he say? You know what they are."

"I know what he is," Dave said dryly. "A witness. Which is something the police don't have. Nobody can say Kerlee was here. Not even you."

"I wasn't feeling well. I lay down upstairs. I fell asleep. I didn't even know Ben had come home."

"Home?" Dave winced up at the sun. "Where had he been?"

"Why, I—" She jerked the card in two. She looked down at it, surprised. She looked at him, afraid. "At—at his office. Yes. The department was his life. He often—"

Dave shook his head. "He hadn't been in. Not since the demonstration, Saturday morning, when Kerlee made his pretty speech. Your husband's absence was unusual enough for his staff to notice. And talk about to a stranger."

"I don't know where he was." She was watching her fingers make fragments of the card. "Can't you"—she looked up with tears in her eyes—"can't you leave it alone? What difference does it make? He's dead. Dead."

"Kerlee isn't," Dave said. "Look, Mrs. Orton—he can't

6

lock his pickup truck. The side windows are broken out. He left the bag lying on the seat. Anyone could have brought it here. Including your husband."

"What?" She scoffed. "Why? It had that petition in it. He'd already refused to take it. That's why Kerlee came. To try to force it on him." Her laugh was grim. "As if Ben could be forced. By a creature like that. There's another one, you know—Richard T. Nowell. A thorn in Ben's side for years. But at least he belongs here. An old La Caleta family. But this maniac Kerlee! Do you know he attacked them when they tried to arrest him? Would an innocent man do that? Oh, it was him, all right. He brought that bag. He brought the flowerpot."

"What became of the pieces?" Dave wondered.

She said, "He kept a crate of them at his place."

"To mix with the soil for drainage," Dave said. "The police went over those. No traces of blood or hair."

"I thought you said they weren't thorough."

"Only about Kerlee," Dave said.

"He owns a nursery. And there were"—the words came shaken, with fury at Dave, with grief for herself—"bits of broken flowerpot embedded in Ben's brain."

"But none in the room. Why not?"

"Why, he cleaned them up, of course. He wouldn't dare leave them. They'd show he'd been here."

"A man so rattled he forgot his tote bag?"

"It had to be him," she said. "It had to."

"That's what the police decided. Mrs. Orton, they didn't even take fingerprints. The only photos in that file were taken to show Kerlee's bag beside the body. He'd threatened to kill your husband. And they went straight after him, no questions asked."

"And who should they have gone after?" She tried for a

7

sneer but missed. There was too much panic in her. Her fingers told about that. They dropped the scraps of card like sad confetti.

"I don't know," he said, "but I'm going to find out. And I'd be grateful if you'd help me. May I look at Chief Orton's den, please?"

"No, you may not!" She stood rigid, chin lifted, the blossom eyes narrowed. "You don't fool me. You don't give a damn about Cliff Kerlee. It's me you're after. And Jerry. We're who your company will have to pay. Unless you can prove one of us killed him."

"Come on, now, Mrs. Orton. You're overexcited."

She didn't hear. She thrust a flushed face up at him. "Well, you never will. Never." Her voice trembled. "I lived my life for Ben Orton. He was everything to me. Ask whoever you like—even people who hated us. Reporters. Daisy Flynn. Ask them. And Jerry? He worshiped his father."

Dave squinted up at the sun again. "What about Anita?" He heard her gasp but he didn't look at her. He looked at the bay. "Her father had her listed too. Twenty-five thousand dollars for each of you. That was how the policy read originally. Then, two years ago, he cut her out of it. Why?" He turned. She wasn't standing there anymore. She'd put the door between them. He heard a bolt crash. While they'd talked, he'd glimpsed behind her a curve of stairway—wrought-iron railings, treads of glazed tile in bright floral patterns. Her heels rattled fast on those tiles now, climbing. Above, someplace, a door slammed.

He trudged back down the drive. Heat came out of the car when he opened the door. He shed the jacket, got in, laid the jacket over the back of the passenger seat, and slammed the door. He wanted it to make a loud noise in the morning stillness. He raced the engine for the same reason.

With a jet of icy air hitting him in the chest from a round vent in the dash, he kicked the parking brake and let the car roll down the road. Around the bend above the cannery he left the car again. This time he shut the door with no more than a click. He climbed among drying weeds and bleached rocks to the top of the rise. A hundred yards off, the housed showed white through a shaggy hedge of eucalyptus trees, old red gums. Chaparral covered the distance. He crouched and started through it.

2

The red gums grew beside a whitewashed adobe wall six feet high. They'd been planted away from it but a long time ago. Their thick pink trunks pushed it now. It would fall soon. But not today. Up to his ankles in tattered brown bark, Dave leaned against the wall to get back his breath. He dragged down the knot of his tie, unbuttoned his shirt collar. Then he jumped, hauled himself up, legged over the wall, and dropped into a patio where it was abruptly cool and moist. The ragged old trees shut out the sun. Banana trees raised split fans above pulpy tropical plants. There were outsize ferns. A fountain helped the dampness. It was low and square. The masonry between its shiny tiles was green with moss.

He was facing the end of a one-story wing of the house. Moss crept up the stucco. Windows with Spanish iron grilles broke the wall. So did French doors set in a shallow arch. He walked around the fountain where goldfish glinted among murky weeds and he tried the latch of the doors. They didn't open. From his wallet he took a slip of metal. It turned the simple lock. He pushed the loose door gingerly and stepped onto deep carpet. In the far wall was a carved door. He went to it and inched it open. The curved tile stairway went up into shafts of sunlight from slot windows. He shut the door quietly. A key stuck out of the lock. He turned it.

He looked at the room. It was chalk white, long and wide. Its ceiling peaked at about fifteen feet. Black rafters crossed it. From one hung a hoop chandelier of hammered black iron. Flags stood in corners—a stars and stripes, a California bear. Over an arched fireplace where the fittings were black hammered iron hung a rack of rifles and shotguns. A glass case held plaques and trophies. Service clubs had saluted Ben Orton. He had been honorary chairman of a fund drive for crippled children. The blind had given him a gold-plated statuette of a seeing-eye dog.

Framed documents hand-lettered on mottled paper took up space on one wall. There were commendations from the National Rifle Association, the Veterans of Foreign Wars, Citizens for Decent Literature. There were also photographs. On the inscribed one of J. Edgar Hoover the ink was fading. In a news picture, Ben Orton stood beside a president among sun-glaring limousines; he was saying something to the president; the president was smiling at a little girl holding flowers. Below this hung a framed letter from a defunct attorney general.

In the center of the room a couch of shiny buttoned cowhide faced a bare coffee table. So did two matching chairs. They looked as if they didn't get sat in much. A chair that looked as if it did stood in back of a broad, glossy desk that held two telephones and a gilt-framed color blowup of Orton and family when the children were around ten and twelve. The desk chair was cowhide too—high back, padded arms. Dave sat in it and swiveled to inspect modular shelves behind the desk. Law books, penal-code books, big glossy books on guns, hunting, game birds. Gifts, probably. They didn't look much handled. Nor the one on ancient Mexican art, either.

A two-way radio took up shelf space. Black plastic, brushed aluminum knobs. Meters. Microphone with coiled cord. *The department was his life.* Dave clicked the power knob and gently eased the gain. Faint crackling, a whisper of far voices. He put an ear to the speaker grille. The messages came frayed. "Out here over the rockpile ... already got me three big ones ... fighting the wind ..." Police calls? In Portuguese accents? "Fog up the coast ... come in, Cape Hedge ... rounding the point ..." Dave blinked at the selector knob. Marine band. Fishing boats. Frowning, he switched off the set.

Turning, his foot nudged a wastebasket. Empty. But a white corner stuck out from under the desk. He bent for it. An envelope. Return address "Los Angeles County Museum of Art." He pushed it into a pocket, rose and went to the arrangement of couch, chairs, table. It didn't match the photos in the report folder. He shifted one of the chairs. Where it had stood the rug was discolored. There was no way to scrub up blood. He kneed aside the other chair, the couch. No more stains. There may have been some on the furniture but the leather was sleek and would wash easily. He knelt and ran a hand over the rug. Clean. He dug fingers into it. No grit. It might be in a vacuum-cleaner bag. Unless the bag was paper or plastic and gone with the trash. He got to his feet.

Doors flanked the shelves behind the desk. He opened

one. Toilet, basin, shower. Blinding white. He shut the door and tried the other. Sand-color police uniforms on hangers. Also civilian suits, a brown tweed, a blue pinstripe. Rack of ties on the door. Badge-mounted caps on the shelf. On the floor, shoes, two pair brown, one black. He groped in corners. No vacuum cleaner. He crouched. What was that behind the shoes? Clothing. Not bundled, not even loosely —just thrown. He dragged out worn Levi's, a ragged Army shirt, a greasy leather hat with floppy brim. Something rattled when he picked these up. He groped back again. A pair of warped sandals with something tangled in their clumsy buckles. A gray wig, curled like wood shavings.

He laid the stuff on the coffee table and sat on the couch. In the left front pocket of the Levi's was a fold of money —a hundred dollars in tens, fives, ones. In the right rear pocket was a pouch of clear plastic. He didn't touch it but he didn't think what was in it was tobacco. He tucked the money back and picked up the shirt. A pair of mirror-finish Polaroid goggles was in one pocket. He kept his fingers off them. In the other pocket something crackled. A letter? He pinched an edge with his nails, drew it out, and unfolded it. Words clipped from magazines were pasted on it. He put on glasses. WE HAVE YOUR DAUGHTER. IF YOU WANT HER BACK SAFE THE PRICE IS $25,000. WE WILL PHONE YOU. He tucked the paper back carefully, put his glasses back into his pocket, gathered up everything and returned it to the closet. He used a handkerchief to wipe knobs, wood, leather where he'd touched them, and to draw shut the French doors.

He went over the wall again and, stooping, ran back through the chaparral. Getting down the slope to his car was clumsy. Dirt leaked into his shoes. But he had emptied them and climbed into the car and started it moving when a brown and white fourdoor with a buggywhip antenna waving at its back and the gold La Caleta police badge painted on its doors came around the foot of the bluff. It climbed straight at him. He slowed. It stopped with its bumper against his. A stocky, blond young man got out of it. He wore a uniform like those in the closet of Ben Orton's den. He came to the window and looked at Dave.

"You the insurance investigator?"

"Brandstetter," Dave said. "Medallion Life." He reached a hand out the window. "And you'd be Jerry Orton."

Orton didn't take the hand. "My mother telephoned me. She says you're asking a lot of questions."

Dave drew the hand back. "I hardly got started."

"You upset her very much. How could you do that? Don't you know what she's been through in the past few days? Haven't you got any imagination?"

"I don't like to use it," Dave said.

Orton squinted. "What the hell does that mean?"

"I need facts, Sergeant. That's why I ask questions."

"The facts are in," Orton said. "Clifford Thomas Kerlee killed my father." He frowned at a steel-cased watch on a thick wrist where gold hairs glinted. "She phoned me fifteen minutes ago. Why are you still here?"

"I was watching the otters," Dave said. "I live in L.A. I don't get up this way often."

"Watch them from someplace else," Orton said. "This is private property."

"Why did your father go out of town?"

"Jesus, you deaf or something?" Orton said. "Cliff Kerlee killed him, stood on the steps of the city hall and waved that stupid fag petition and yelled right into the cameras he was

14

going to kill him and he killed him. Man—what are you trying to do—smear my father?"

"That wouldn't accomplish anything," Dave said.

Orton's laugh was sharp and short. "You goddam right it wouldn't. He was one of the outstanding lawmen in this country. He was nominated to head the FBI when Hoover died. Hoover was a friend of his."

"Where did he go when he left town?" Dave asked.

"Get out of that car," Orton said. "Stand up when you talk to a police officer."

Dave got out. The sunlight crashed and shattered on the waves beyond the cannery. Dave winced against the glare. "How far did he go? How long was he gone?"

"Last time he went anywhere for more than a day was Dallas last fall. American Association of Police Chiefs convention. He was a past president."

"He didn't stop into his office the day he was killed. Your mother doesn't know where he was."

"So?" Orton's clean square hand rested on a holster at his hip. A big revolver hung there. "He was out. He came home. Kerlee was waiting for him on the patio."

"Oh? Why the patio?"

"No trouble to get in. Dad didn't worry about security. Figured his reputation would keep prowlers off. There's a lot of overgrown plants there. He could hide easy. Somebody was there. Water from the fountain was splashed around."

"No empty flowerpots?" Dave asked.

"He wouldn't need one. He brought a whole truckload. Patio French doors were open. Patio gate. Door to the inside of the house was locked. My father wouldn't do that. Lock any of us out. He wasn't like that. No secrets."

Dave let his face show small surprise. "He wouldn't work a case alone?"

Orton snorted. "What for? He had twenty men."

"Not even a big case? Try to crack it by himself? Somebody bringing in marijuana by ship?"

Orton half turned his head, looked from the corners of his eyes. "What the hell are you talking about?"

"Just wondering where he went that day. Your mother said the department was his life. I thought he might have been on police business. You don't know where he was?"

"I know where you're going to be. Locked up. For trespassing." Orton jerked his chin. "Get away from here. And stay away."

Dave shrugged, pulled open the door, sat back of the wheel. "I go where the job takes me." He shut the door.

Orton's voice came dim through the glass. "Your only job around here is to get my mother the insurance check that's coming to her." He turned on his heel and started back to the brown and white car.

Dave touched a switch. The window beside him rolled down. He called, "Your father didn't leave her anything?"

Orton stopped, turned. "His pension. No savings." He lifted a hand toward the town that couldn't be seen from here. "He didn't have to hang on in La Caleta and take their nickels and dimes. He had offers, big offers. But he said he didn't want paperwork, he wanted police work." Orton lifted blond eyebrows. "Ah, what the hell. La Caleta's a good town—or was, right up to lately."

"And what went wrong with it lately?"

"Garbage from L.A., from Haight-Ashbury. Hippies, druggies, smutty books, dirty movies, lousy underground newspaper. You know. Pretty little town. What else have they got to do but filthy it up? But"—he blew out a grim

16

sigh—"at least he could control it here. You get up to Frisco or down to L.A. or someplace, a cop doesn't stand a chance. They've got crime up the ass but whose fault is it? The chief of police. Naw—Dad was right. He was always right."

"But it didn't pay," Dave said.

"Get lost," Orton said. His shoes swished in the dry roadside weeds. He got into the police car and slammed the door, and the worn-out engine thrashed in the sun-bright stillness. He backed the car. The transmission was noisy. He jerked the lever to low and crawled past Dave. Dave shouted above the racket of loose valves:

"Where is your sister, Sergeant?"

Orton braked. His face twisted. "What? Why?"

"I just wondered if you knew."

"Hell, yes, I know. What's it to you?"

"Your mother seems worried about her."

"You're out of your mind." Orton's car jerked and stalled. He started it again angrily. "She's at school. College. Sangre de Cristo State." He roared off. The smoke of his going hung sullen in the motionless air.

3

South from La Caleta, Highway 1 cuts inland. He drove between hills parched after a short winter of scant rain. Whiteface cattle browsed the tawny grass, made lazy paths up the rutted sides of barrancas, drank at wooden tanks. There were clumps of green live-oaks. In their shadows, horses stood nooning, neck over neck. A leggy colt raced beside a barbwire fence. Ranch buildings nestled at the foot of a towering rock outcrop. In the yard a tiny figure pushed bales off a red pickup truck. Beside the road someone had painted JESUS on a rock. Motels began to advertise. When he reached the metal tree of welcomes to Sangre de Cristo from Kiwanis, Elks, Rotary, he checked his watch. Not quite eleven. It wasn't all that far.

The town baked in a surround of brown hills. He drove sleepy streets with no sidewalks, where frame houses with slim windows and jigsaw-work porches stood up straight under old trees. He came to a street of cinderblock warehouses. Then there was the railroad station—arches, red tile roof, boxcars waiting on sidings. He jounced across four sets of tracks, and the road went steeply up. Ahead of him, the double rear tires of a bus stirred yellow dust from the road shoulder. The bus halted at a break in a plastered adobe wall that shut off a yard dark with eucalyptus. At the top of an arch, a green bronze bell hung above heavy plank gates. Out of the bus clambered middle-aged women in flowered dresses and sunglasses. Carrying cameras and guidebooks, they clustered around a signboard lettered with the history of Sangre de Cristo mission. He drove around the bus.

Sangre de Cristo State College took up a lot of good grazing land above town so it could space its buildings far apart. They were poured concrete, rock conglomerate, and smoky glass. They looked lonely in the sun. No one was in the parking-lot gatehouse. A guitar hung there. A textbook lay face down on a stool. But no one appeared. Maybe because the parking lot was full. After he'd cruised every rank he left and tried another driveway farther on. FACULTY ONLY. Here flowering succulents struggled in planter strips between the rows of cars. He found a slot whose curb was stenciled MR. ROWBOTHAM and left the Electra in it. He hoped it was Rowbotham's day off.

The campus walks were glaring white and straight and very long. Sprinkler systems made rainbows between them but the lawns played dead. The sun struck down. He had buttoned his shirt collar and fixed his tie and put on his jacket. Now he took off the jacket again. A thin girl with long pale hair rode a bicycle past him, books balanced on the handlebars. When he asked her, she pointed out the administration building without stopping. It was a long way off. He loosened tie and collar again. Sweat trickled down his ribs. Sweat trickled out of his hair into his eyes. No wonder so few students were around.

In neat concrete boxes Brazilian pepper trees grew at the foot of long, broad, white terraces that led up to the administration building. The trees looked new, like everything else here. Except himself. Seen in the wavy dark glass of the doors, he looked ragged. The air conditioning was icy inside. The woman behind the information counter wore wool, a yellow pants suit. Her glasses were very large, very round, with yellow frames. Quite a while ago a surgeon had yanked the sag ⁓ut of her face, but it was back. Expression wasn't, but maybe there'd never been any. He gave her a smile and showed her the identification in his wallet. Tucking the wallet back into the jacket over his arm, he lied:

"I need to see Anita Orton, please. It's about her father's life-insurance policy. Her late father."

"Is she registered here?"

"No, she's registered in Florida but this is closer."

The eyes behind the saucer lenses were baleful but only a twitch of her mouth answered. She went into an office where a long-haired boy sat pushing typewriter keys with one hand while he drank from a Coke can in the other. Dave heard file drawers slam. The woman in yellow came back with an index card. "She has no classes today. You'd have to look for her at home."

"You don't mean in La Caleta?" Dave asked.

She meant rooms above the stables of a hulking old mansion with verandas and turrets and stained glass on a deep corner lot near the mission. The trees were gloomy acacias and magnolias. On the patchy grass under them lay bicycles. The oak front door stood open and rock music drifted out on the hot air. A girl in half a bikini lay asleep facedown

20

on the green composition shingles of a side porch. Her skin was rich gold and glossy with suntan oil. Dave swung the Electra up the drive. New small cars, large old cars, motorcycles, motor scooters crowded the stable yard in back. The stable building itself was sided in scalloped shingles. Its paint, like the paint of the house, was yellowing. He climbed an outside staircase. When he rapped a screen door at the top a little dog yapped.

"Frodo!" a girl's voice called. "Knock it off." The girl came to the door, wrapping long dark hair in a towel. She wore bib overalls. The little dog jumped at the screen like a fur yo-yo. "Who are you?"

He told her. "I'm looking for Anita Orton."

"She's not here—sorry."

"Can you tell me where to find her?"

"You look beat." She pushed open the door. The dog growled around Dave's shoes. "Frodo, no," the girl said, and to Dave, "Come in. I've made shrub." She went away down a long room bright with strewn record albums and paperback books and green with potted plants hung from the ceiling by frizzy ropes in fancy colors, fancy knots and tassles. "You'll like it. It's not sweet." Glass and ice cubes rattled afar. Dave sat on denim cushions on the floor. They were big cushions and crazily embroidered. She came back with the towel made into a turban and handed him a glass of murky brown liquid. "Try it. Don't be afraid."

He tried it. It wasn't sweet.

"Herbs." She sat cross-legged in front of him on the stitched-together squares of grass matting that covered the floor. "Anita got a phone call." She waved at a gold and ivory instrument out of a Mae West boudoir. "Gee—it's been ten days or something. In the morning. She threw stuff in a bag and left. It was some dude."

"Maybe it was her father," Dave said.

She had a mouthful of shrub. She gave a quick swallow, shook her head. "No. He was here. A couple of days later. Like you." She tried to make her young voice gruff. " 'I'm looking for Anita Orton.' Only not like you. You're pretty."

"Wearing Levi's, an old Army shirt, shades?"

Her eyes opened wide. "You're kidding." She stuck out her chest and saluted. "Uniform. Badge. Big gun. A gun is a substitute penis. Did you know that?"

"I didn't go to college," Dave said. "The voice on the telephone?"

"Black," she said. "I didn't think about it till he asked me—the Big Chief, I mean. He said, 'Did it sound like a Negro?' I said, 'Yeah, maybe.' But it did. I'm sure of it now."

"She didn't tell you his name or where she was going?"

The girl frowned and poked at the ice cubes in her glass. "And he was dead only two days later. You wouldn't think it could happen to somebody like that. I mean, he looked like he was made out of iron or something." She twitched Dave a skeptical smile. "Oh, I know it's role playing and all that." Her naked shoulders moved under the overall straps. "But you believe, you know? They say, 'I am *the chief*,' you know? And you say, 'Yup, yessir, you de chief' —right?" She laughed, set the glass down, jumped up and vanished again among the hanging plants. She called, "They have a sweet sound, you know? When they're trying not to sound sleepy-time down south?" A refrigerator door clapped on its rubber stripping. "Sweet and elegant and a little faggoty?"

"Police chiefs?" Dave called.

"Blacks, you nut." She came back carrying wooden bowls of salad, bounced down in her lotus position again, and handed one of the bowls to Dave. The dog scratched at the screen. "Lunch," she said. "All organic. The kids in agro grow it. Bug pickers. They really get sunburned. I think there'll be a new generation of insecticide fans." She dug into the salad. But with a forkful of alfalfa sprouts halfway to her mouth she stopped moving and her eyes opened wide again. "It was a faggot who killed him, wasn't it?"

"So they say," Dave said. "But not black." The bowl had been chilling. He liked that idea and tried the salad. It was crisp and bland. "How did she react to the phone call? Did it frighten her?"

"Frighten? Oh, no. It was like light bulbs went on inside her." The little dog whined at the screen. "Cool it, Frodo." She chewed reflectively. "Come to think of it, that was the first time I ever saw her really happy."

"It wasn't some boyfriend you'd met?" Dave asked.

"She didn't have boyfriends. She just studied and sulked. Like she was waiting for something. Ages."

"Did she write letters?" Dave asked.

"Mmm." The girl nodded with her mouth full. She washed down the salad with a long swallow of shrub, then went to let in the dog. Claws rattly on the grass mats, he followed her to the kitchen. The bowl knocked wooden on the floor. A vegetarian dog? "She wrote a letter almost every day."

"To whom?" Dave called.

The girl came halfway back and stood looking at him from between the plants. "It was a big secret. If you came in and she was typing, she covered up the paper." The little dog yapped and jumped around her legs. She worked an opener on a can labelled FRISKIES. Not a vegetarian dog. "I mean, how sexist can you get? Who cared who she was writing to? I mean, it's such a stereotype, you know?" She went back into the kitchen. "The curious female? Eve? Pandora? Bluebeard's wife? What kind of mind thinks like that anymore?" The dog stopped barking.

"What about answers?" Dave called.

"From Soledad." The girl came back, wiping her hands on the overall bib. "A post-office box number. If the mail was late, I'd bring it up. Out of the mailbox at the foot of the stairs. But only if she was at school. Ninety percent of the time, she was down there waiting for it."

"You don't remember a name?" Dave said.

She looked at the ceiling and tried a name out. "Lester? Lester—yeah." She gave up, sighed, sat down, shook her head. "I really didn't care," she said.

"I believe you," Dave said. He ate his salad.

"Insurance investigator?" She studied him. "That's like a detective, isn't it?"

He gave her a little smile.

"And you're here now." She unwrapped her hair and began to scrub it with the towel. "So you don't think who they say did it, did it. Yeah, that's what you said."

"She drive a car?" Dave asked.

"A bright green Gremlin. Brand new, just got it."

"Her father came here. Who else?"

"TV newspeople. The night he was killed." She let the towel fall and shook out her hair. "Do you think Anita killed him?"

"I don't know what to think. You knew her. What do you think?"

"Only for a year." The girl crossed the matting on hands and knees. Back of the flossy telephone, a mirror in a gold lace frame leaned against the wall. Combs and brushes lay there, a hot-air blower. She turned it on. It whined. She

24

pointed it at her head and began to comb, wincing. "She's got a United Farm Workers poster on her wall, you know?" She quit with the blower and hoisted and swung an imaginary banner on a pole. *"Viva la huelga!"* She scowled, a rebel girl, then gave a little wondering laugh and went back to blowing and combing. "And she lies on her bed under it, reading the recipes in *Family Circle.*"

"What TV newspeople?" Dave asked.

"That withered hag from Channel Ten. Daisy Flynn. With a potbellied cameraman. Ghouls. They were really disappointed she wasn't here. They wanted her to cry for them."

"And would she have cried?" Dave set down his bowl.

"You're kidding," the girl said. "She hated him."

4

The building didn't need style or windows. It was square-cornered cement block and it stood between tall steel latticework towers on top of a mountain all alone. On its roof reared ten-foot-high letters in red, white, and blue stripes. KSDC-TV. Maybe they were readable from the town below. Nine vehicles nosed the building. He ran the Electra in between a Honda Civic and a Ford van and got out. The silence was total. A cry made a cut in it. He looked up. A hawk circled against the sun. He thought, *He could be dead by now.* It was a useless thought. He pushed a door where the red, white, and blue letters repeated themselves and a faded bumper sticker peeled—CHANNEL 10 LOOK AGAIN.

On the other side of the door, ranch-house chairs and couches slumped under clumsy paintings of cattle and red-rock sunsets. A low table had thumbed magazines and coffee-cup rings on it. A red motorcycle bounced noiseless off a dusty hilltop on a television screen. On a desk at which no one sat, a big, slope-fronted, multibutton telephone winked to itself. Dave shouldered a heavy, hand-smudged door that wheezed. Down a hallway cluttered with microphone booms and camera dollies, men in pastel shirts bunched, telling jokes. They held papers and plastic cups. One of them saw Dave and came to him, stepping over thick cables that snaked the floor. His face was brick-color. Makeup. He took Dave to Daisy Flynn.

She wasn't a withered hag. She just hadn't been a college girl for a long time. She sat in a room stacked and racked with canned film. Film turned on reels in front of her, showing her images, frame by frame, on a screen tilted hopefully upward like a child's bright face. Typed pages lay beside her and a hand bony like the rest of her crossed out sentences with a felt-tip pen. The surprised eyes she raised to him had blue paint above them. She pushed glasses up onto red-tinted hair. A disbelieving smile dug lines around her mouth. She had television teeth.

"Louise Orton said to ask me?"

Dave nodded. "She said 'even' you. Was she devoted to him?"

"Mindlessly." Daisy Flynn switched off the editing machine. To a man standing in a corner squinting at loops and streamers of film, she called, "Burt, love, cut this where I've marked it, will you?" She picked up the papers and led Dave down a hallway, then through a shadowy cavern where spotlights hung from steel rafters, where cameras stood around and microphones glinted and sleek curved desks and fake paneled walls waited for the clock, the next news slot, candidate interview, land-development commercial. She moved fast, like everyone in the flat-lighted room they ended up in—typewriters, jangling phones, stuttering teletypes. "Sit down," she said. "Coffee?"

27

"You're working. I don't want to keep you." He glanced over his shoulder. "Have you got film in there of the Orton funeral?"

"Would we have missed it?" She sat down. "You're working too but I do want to keep you. For that very reason. What brings you around, Mr. Brandstetter? I mean —what were you doing chatting with the widow? Insurance, you said. And you wanted to know whether she really loved him or not. You aren't happy with the verdict?"

"The verdict isn't in." Dave sat opposite her.

"Ho!" She chuckled. "You don't know La Caleta." Out of a drawer she brought a hand-size box of chrome and white plastic. A cassette recorder. She pressed buttons and set it on the desk. "We'll get a camera later."

Dave switched the thing off. "This isn't a news story, Miss Flynn. Where a policyholder meets a violent death, every insurance company investigates. It's routine."

She looked at the machine. She looked at him, her mouth pursed. "Of course it is. That's why you're driving all over the landscape to talk to peripheral characters like me. I may be peripheral, but I'm quick."

Dave shrugged. "Nothing in it. I like my work. It's a handsome landscape. And you have film."

"Yards and yards." She messed among papers. They were all like the ones she'd brought back from the editing room—typed down half the page in capital letters. She found a pack of cigarettes and pushed it at him. "We take —took—an intense interest in Ben Orton. This is salt-of-the-earth country. Ben Orton was its hero." She watched him take a cigarette, took one herself. The air conditioner blew hard but he managed to light them both.

" 'Mindlessly'?" He pushed the narrow steel lighter back

28

into his shirt pocket. "Does that mean you think her faith in him was misplaced?"

"It means that's the kind of woman she is," Daisy Flynn said. "It also means Ben Orton wasn't just a police chief— he was also a man." She looked up with a mechanical smile at a skinny black youth who set down a yellow tray on which plastic holders gripped paper cups of coffee. "And that women, too, worship heroes. Thank you, Cecil. Will you pull all the recent footage on Ben Orton, please? Mr. Brandstetter here wants to look at it." He nodded, grinned, and walked off.

Dave looked after him. He hadn't seen another black all day. "Channel Ten's token?" he asked.

"This isn't exactly Tanzania," she said. "He's in communications arts at the college. Senior students rotate through here. For working experience. We get state funds for the program. God knows what they learn. It probably warps them for life."

"He makes fair coffee," Dave said. But maybe after the shrub anything would have tasted good. "His last name wouldn't be Lester, would it?"

She was using shiny red talons to tear open little envelopes of sugar and cream substitute. The question made her stop moving for a split second. Then she said lightly, "It would be Harris." She stirred her coffee with a plastic spoon. "Why the funeral? I mean, that's a bit after the fact, isn't it?"

"It can sometimes help to see who was there. You went down to interview Anita after the fact—right?"

"You have been busy!" She said it lightly but her eyes went watchful. "We have a little news bureau in La Caleta. When they learned Ben Orton had been murdered, I expect there was quite a scramble to get out of swim fins and into shoes. They had plenty to do."

"So did the police," Dave said. "They didn't do it."

Daisy Flynn twitched an eyebrow. Her hand moved to the tape recorder again but stopped when she saw him watching it. She said, "Anyway, I was up here. So was Anita."

"Only she wasn't," Dave said.

Daisy Flynn found a glass ashtray and set it between them. "She'd only have made a footnote anyway." She poked her cigarette among the lipsticked butts already there. "What do you want with her?"

"I don't know. I didn't find her, either," Dave said. "So . . . Orton had other women, did he?"

Daisy Flynn's eyes opened wide above her paper cup. "Did I say that?" She sipped the creamy coffee. "Let's put it this way—if he did, it was a well-kept secret."

A bearded youth clutching a scribbled yellow pad and flapping into a jacket hurried past, trailed by a paunchy man swinging a movie camera with a padded shoulder saddle. They pushed out a door into stunning sunlight. Before the door had time to fall shut, car doors slammed, an engine thrashed into life.

Dave asked, "From them? From your viewers—the lonely ranch hands in their bunkhouses back in the hills? The wine bottlers? The tuna-fleet wives? The college kids?" He eyed her steadily. "Or from you?"

"What Ben Orton wanted kept secret was kept secret," she said flatly. "He had what's politely called power. There are nastier words for it." She moved a hand to get rid of the subject. "The point is, Louise would have been the last to know."

"Because he could destroy anyone who told her?"

"And she wouldn't believe them anyway," Daisy Flynn said. "You met her. You're bright. You saw that."

"Maybe," Dave said. "But nobody likes to be made a fool of. Certainly not for a lifetime."

She stared. "You can't believe she'd kill him."

"She was alone in the house with him."

Daisy Flynn crushed out her cigarette. Her laugh was mournful. "That's a real definition of 'alone.' " She looked up quickly. "Or so I would imagine."

"She has a little list," Dave said. "Radicals, dope addicts, degenerates—and reporters. You in particular and by name. Why?"

"We filmed his public utterances." She rose. "As you, lucky fellow, are about to see." Dave stood, tossed back the last of his coffee, and followed her between the crowded desks, frantic humans, frantic phones, frantic typewriters. "He always ended up appearing ridiculous." The hush of the hallway shocked Dave's ears. "She couldn't understand why people laughed. I'm sure she never laughed." Daisy Flynn pushed a door. Back of it was a shadowy room. Up a sharp rise, nine theater seats faced a blank white screen. "It had to be someone's fault. It must have been ours—right?"

"Film can be manipulated," Dave said.

"It wasn't—not here." Light leaked from slot windows in a projection booth up short stairs and behind the seats. She called, "Cecil, baby, are you there?"

"All set up." Cecil's voice came muffled.

"The men who own this mountain, this building, and all that is therein also own most of the landscape you so much admired between here and La Caleta. Ranchers, growers, vintners. Rich and loud. They liked Orton."

Light shafted from the projection booth. On the screen,

31

numbers inside targets flickered upside down.

"So you didn't switch Ben Orton footage around?"

"Not if I wanted to go on eating." She tinkered with a digital watch on a bony wrist. She peered at it. "Which I won't do if I don't get a move on."

"If they liked him, why didn't they see to it he got paid? Did you know he died broke?"

Colors reflected from the screen made her frown garish. "No. I mean, twenty-five thousand a year isn't half bad out here in the boondocks. He lived, as they say, simply. Nobody ever accused him of extravagance." She gave her head a quick, troubled shake and opened the room door. "Enjoy," she told him with a tight smile. "And see me before you leave—all right?"

"Wait," he said. "Who laughed at him?"

"Anyone with an I.Q. over ninety." She went away.

5

On the screen, long-haired lads in tank tops and faded bellbottom jeans carried picket signs in front of a white, sunstruck building marked LA CALETA CITY HALL. Dave dropped into a seat. A lot of the lads had muscles but they minced. There appeared to be chatting and laughter. At a guess, high-pitched. Someone pirouetted. A shriek would have gone with that. The camera moved in. They weren't all lads. Thin hair stirred on a bald scalp. A beer belly bulged through a fringed leather vest.

"You want the sound, Mr. Bannister?" Cecil stood at his shoulder.

"I can imagine it, thanks," Dave said.

" 'Five, six, seven, eight—,' " Cecil grinned.

" '—Gay is just as good as straight,' " Dave said.

"Do they all want to be cops?" Cecil asked.

"They all want to be girls," Dave said. "But it's the principle of the thing."

The screen filled with a placard lettered in orange marker pen, NEANDERTHAL GO HOME. It wobbled. The next frames showed a pair of sturdy youths in sand-color uniforms standing, feet apart, hands behind their backs, at the top of the city hall's tidy front steps. A doorway was a black, rectangular hole behind them. Sun glinted off their short fair hair, their badges, their sunglasses. They wore heavy guns and nightsticks and no expression.

Not even when the picket signs surged toward them. They didn't move. They stood blocking the door. The first of the demonstrators charged up the steps. The camera tilted. The signs waved. It was hard to read them. GAY. LAW & ORDER. EQUALITY. GERMS. Germs? What was that about? A blur of red and yellow doubleknit stripes blocked the camera. Then it was clear again and watching from another angle. At the top of the steps, a gaunt man, beard, mustache, yellow hair clubbed back, sweaty blue workshirt with the arms torn off, flapped long sheets of paper in front of the stoical cops. They stared straight ahead.

Behind them in the shadowed doorway a face made a pale, square blur. Ben Orton? The gaunt man lunged. The uniformed boys caught him. He seemed to be kicking. One of the officers raised a nightstick. A sign slammed him between the shoulders. It said something about FREEDOM. Bodies got in the camera's way. There was a splice in the film. The cameraman had switched to telephoto. The gaunt man's face filled the screen. Blood trickled down a forehead where a ropy vein swelled. Framed by the tobacco-stained beard, his teeth were rabbity. His eyes bulged. He raved.

Dave asked, "Could I just have the sound on this?"

Cecil went away. The screen became a streak of color. The film jerked and froze at the frame with the lifted nightstick. The film rolled. All the sound was screaming. Yes, that was Ben Orton in the doorway. What Cliff Kerlee shouted was "... legal petition from the voters, taxpayers, citizens of this community. What does he mean—refuse? Who the hell does he think he is?" He struggled in the hands of the officers. Tendons stood out in his scrawny neck. The cameraman focused on the steps where deck shoes, rubber sandals, dirty bare feet trampled the long pages of ballpoint signatures. Kerlee screamed, "Pig! Arrogant straight! I'll kill the fat—" An electronic tone replaced the words writhing out of the beard. Kerlee went down out of sight. Signs and shaggy heads shifted. And then there were the target numbers again and the bright white blankness of the screen.

"Thanks," Dave called.

"There's more," Cecil answered. "Just a second."

It was out of chronological order. A week earlier? He'd heard of it but that was all. Microphones poked at Ben Orton's square jaw. He wore a cap with a badge on it. The gold-braided bill cast a shadow in the harsh sunlight. He jerked slightly with surprise and took off the cap. His hair was close cropped. And his mustache. Both gray. The television people had backgrounded him with a hibiscus bush. The red flowers looked as if they were reaching for him. His voice was outdoor high with a whine to it.

"People wouldn't sign these petitions if they knew what homosexuals are really like. Police officers know that—how these weirdos live their lives. Alleys. Public toilets. Back rows of dirty theaters. What they do—with men they never saw before. Anybody. It's not just that they're mentally sick. They spread germs. You get people like that in your police-department locker rooms—you could have your whole police force down with venereal disease. Is that what the people want that are signing these petitions? Well, I can

35

tell you, it's not what the police officers want—or their wives."

Someone unseen interrupted with a question. The wind took it away before the microphones could catch it. Whether Orton heard it was impossible to tell. He said:

"Leave that out if you want to. The whole idea is ridiculous, any way you look at it. What man you know is going to want to be stuck in a patrol car eight hours a day with some pervert? And suppose there's trouble—and trouble is what that patrol car is out there to stop. Can you picture some homosexual charging a house where some crazy is shooting guns out the window? I'd hate to see the face of the mother who's signing one of these petitions today when she finds out later a homosexual police officer has been sent to find her lost six-year-old son."

Dave unfolded from his seat, went up the short aisle and the short steps, and looked into the projection booth. Cecil was hunched on a green metal stool in the small work light of one of the projectors, reading a paperback book on electronic journalism. Out in the tinted darkness, the voice of Ben Orton went on: "That mother isn't going to thank Sacramento for passing that bill. She isn't going to thank the city attorney for enforcing it. She isn't going to thank the Civil Service Commission that made me put that queer into a job where—." Dave said, "I came for the funeral. The build-up is good but it's too long."

Cecil laughed, tossed the book away, got off the stool, and sped up the reels of the projector. A loose end of film flapped. He knocked a switch and touched the wound-up reel with a long, pale-palmed hand until it quit spinning. He jerked the reel off the machine and dropped it noisily into a can. "One funeral, coming up," he said, and pried the lid off another can.

Dave went back to his seat. But what came up this time was Daisy Flynn seated in a little blue armchair between Cliff Kerlee, in a jumpsuit, and a gray-haired man Dave thought he knew, who wore a hand-loomed tweed jacket and went to an expensive barber. The camera dollied in on Daisy Flynn. She said, "Today we're talking with two leaders of the local gay community, Richard T. Nowell, who began his work in 1953, and Cliff Kerlee, founder of Gay Action." Smile. "Gentlemen, I know your reactions to Police Chief Ben Orton's statement that we've just seen differ. How and why? Dick Nowell, will you start?" Cecil yelped from the booth. The film streaked past.

Dave lit a cigarette in the dark and groped for and found the flip-up metal lid of a little ashtray in the arm of his seat. The screen took color again. The setting was as he'd remembered it—brown hump hills in the distance, in the foreground half-grown shade trees, plaques in the grass, long lines of uniformed men standing at attention, women in quiet clothes and gloves and hats, seated on metal folding chairs that faced a gunmetal coffin blanketed by a flag. Wreaths on easels. White wicker holders for tall sprays of gladiolus. A rank of rifles raised, jerking puffs of smoke. A bugler wincing into a twist of brass. The long, involved ceremonial folding of the coffin flag, its delivery into the hands of the widow. Uniformed son standing woodenly behind her chair. Tears leaking from under his dark glasses.

Dave thought, *Christ, I don't even know what he wants. To be buried? Where? Maybe Amanda knows. No. He'd never talk death to Amanda.*

Dave called to Cecil, "Can you stop it there?" It stopped. A blond young woman on a chair next to Louise Orton had lifted her hand, turned her head, raised it slightly. "Now can you roll it very slowly?" It jerked ahead, frame by frame. The young woman's hand inched upward. It found Jerry Orton's hand, which rested on his mother's shoulder. The young woman's look searched the young man's face. It was a tender look. "Hold it there, please?" The film stopped, the screen went dark. Cecil came out of the booth. Dave asked him, "That woman—do you know? Was that Anita Orton?"

Cecil shook his head. "No way."

"It's a big school," Dave said, "and very white."

"That's how I know. Black, you know all the blacks. I don't mean know, but know—you know? And year before last, Anita Orton went with a black boy."

"Lester," Dave said.

"Lester Green," Cecil said. "He made a mistake. Not a little mistake, a big mistake."

"And ended up in prison at Soledad," Dave said.

"She was nobody to fool with. Lester said, 'I'm not fooling.' Neither was her daddy. Five years for possession. Shit, Lester never blew pot. He wouldn't stay in a room with it. No, that is not Anita Orton."

"I didn't think it would be." Dave stood up. "How crazy was he?"

Cecil twisted his face. "Crazy? Lester? He was so square he couldn't turn over in bed."

"He never wanted to burn it all down?"

Cecil faked indignation, popped his eyes, flared his nostrils. " 'Listen to me, man—I am a *law* student.' " He made his mouth very round on the word. " 'The *law* is *it*— understand me?' "

Dave said, "He didn't know there were two kinds?"

"One for the rich and one for the poor? He does now," Cecil said.

"Maybe it changed him. Where did he live—family?"

"La Caleta. Mama was all, far as I know. The kind that tied her hair up in a rag and scrubbed white folks's kitchens, so Lester could become Thurgood Marshall."

"I appreciate your help."

"Any time." Cecil started for the booth. "He out?"

"Five years can mean two"—Dave pushed the door—"with good behavior."

"Oh, Lester would be good," Cecil said.

"And you?" Dave held the door. "Miss Flynn thinks there's a news story in this. Don't get her excited."

Cecil stood in the projection-booth doorway. The light was behind him but his teeth showed. "If it's a beat," he said, "it's my beat."

"It's not a beat," Dave said. "Not yet."

He let the door fall shut and went back along the soundproof hallway. She wasn't at her desk. She was on the air. He watched her through double panes of glass from a dim, narrow room walled with busy picture tubes tended by a man in earphones whose hands moved on switches and slide controls. Out in the studio, the silhouetted floor people, directors, and technicians stood among hulking cameras like marionettes strung with fallen wires. Beyond them, at the curved desk, newscasters sat in shafts of light. The men shuffled papers, smiled at the cameras. Daisy Flynn's dye job flared. Her face was suddenly on all the monitors. Her voice came out of loudspeakers above Dave's head. She said:

"And finally, a Channel Ten Newsdesk exclusive. A new development in the bludgeoning death last week of Police Chief Benjamin J. Orton of La Caleta. Medallion of Los Angeles, the company that insured Chief Orton's life, is busy today interviewing persons connected with the case. Death-claims investigator David Brandstetter declined to be taped or photographed and told this reporter his inquiries were simply routine. But he did express doubt that Clifford Thomas Kerlee, the gay-activist leader now in jail awaiting trial for Chief Orton's murder, is guilty of that killing." She paused, then smiled. "And now, good afternoon from all of us here at Channel Ten's Newsdesk."

The screens showed a blue plastic bottle of detergent, lighted and filmed with reverence. He pushed out of the control room. He yanked open the twin doors to the studio. She came out of the harsh lights into the shadows. She was laughing between the two men. When she saw Dave, she stopped—stopped laughing, stopped walking. The two men glanced at her, at him, and went on past. Dave told her, "I said I wasn't a story."

"I've been in this business a long time," she said. "Don't you think I know a story when I see it?"

"Quick enough to kill it," Dave said.

"The people have a right to know," she said.

"People who murder other people give up a lot of rights," Dave said. "Someone out there was breathing easy, walking around smiling, sure that Kerlee would get it for what he did. Now what's he doing?"

"You'll get him," she said. "Or her. I checked you out with the L.A. police. You're the best in your game."

"Except it's not a game," Dave said. "Can you find me a photo of Ben Orton?"

"If I do, will you forgive me?" She said it archly and dropped some of her script. The pages whispered across dusty black vinyl tile. He let them lie there.

"You'd just do it again," he said.

"I'll do it again"—she stooped for the papers—"in any case." She rose. "Come with me."

40

The California Adult Authority had offices in a flat-roofed building that smelled new inside. GEORGE ANDERSON was the name cut into a wedge of polished wood on the desk in the office he was sent to. Anderson said, "Lester Green got out on the sixteenth and reported to me. Phoned in a week later. He's living with his mother in La Caleta."

A wide window gave a view of the parking lot. "That's nice," Dave said. "Did you see how he got here?"

"A blond girl brought him," Anderson said. "A little bit fat. In a brand-new, bright green Gremlin."

6

Shopfronts of raw planks faced the bay. A crooked wooden deck followed the curve of the shore and hung over the water. Its railings were two-by-fours painted white. Sets of board steps painted white dropped maybe ten feet to moorings where sail and power pleasurecraft bumped clean gunwales. Farther out on the bright blue water, bigger boats rocked at anchor—slim ketches, scarred fishing boats, launches lofty with superstructure. Under slices of colored sail, skiffs tilted, filled with kids.

Widows in sunhats and sleeveless dresses sipped chilled white wine and ate sole in cream sauce at shaded tables in front of a restaurant whose sign pictured a cartoon fish in a sombrero. The place called itself El Pescadero. The sign on the next shop was shaped like a palette and promised ART SUPPLIES, but the door was locked. He rattled it. No one came. He shaded his eyes with his hands and peered through the window. Reflections off the water rippled on the ceiling. Bad seascapes repeated themselves on walls covered with burlap. No one stirred.

His mouth tightened and he turned away. He'd just come from another locked door. Ophelia R. Green's, 127 Poppy Street, one of a straggle of shacks under heavy-headed old pepper trees in a tuck of the hills on the far side of the highway. He'd rapped a door that was a flimsy wooden frame for bulging squares of screen. He'd waited on the warped boards of a little stoop in the hot sun. When she hadn't come, he'd walked around back where the yard went up steeply. Flowers smiled. There were tidy rows of cabbages, onions, tomato plants. A slap-up garage was half dug into the slope. Its door scraped weedy ground when he pulled it open. Bunches of dried flower bulbs hung from the rafters, trailing tatters of brown paper sacking. Underfoot not an oil leak or tire track showed that a car had ever sheltered here. Against a wall leaned a motorcycle covered by a tarp. Dust rose sluggishly and made him cough when he lifted the tarp. The machine was shiny but its tires were flat. He went out into the sunlight again and shut the weary door. A screen porch hung off the back of the house. He climbed three steps and peered inside. A washing machine stood there, the old kind with wringers. Rumpled clothes lay on top of it, jockey shorts, tank tops, jeans. He went down the steps. In the next yard, where tall hollyhocks swayed, a shriveled Mexican woman milked a goat. Dave asked her in Spanish where *la Señora Green* was. *La Negra* cleaned the house of someone unknown. She would be home at supper time. *La hora de cenar* ...

He'd like to have seen her first. But he could use the afternoon. If he could find paints. He went down a passageway into a patio where a jacaranda tree spread feathery shade and strewed the red paving tiles with blue blossom.

The shops facing the tree had been fitted with raw wooden fronts too. From their exposed rafter ends fishnets hung in swags. Panchos, serapes, small rugs made color in one window. The framework of a loom rose behind them. In the next window, handcrafted silver set with turquoise lay on artfully crumpled velvet. A third window showed hand-tooled leather goods—sandals, bags, belts.

In a window in a corner, watercolors hung against a panel covered in monk's cloth. The subjects were predictable—boats, gulls, rickety piers. He made the locus Monterey. But the drawing and brushwork were better than good and the eye had seen honestly. Above the pictures a signature was brushed large on a card—*Tyree Smith.* On the window glass, fresh gilt lettering read MONA WINDROW GALLERY. The signboard overhead had been painted out with white but he could see what had been lettered on it: BEACHCOMBER—COMPLETE LINE OF ARTISTS NEEDS. Had been. He shrugged and went inside.

The walls were freshly painted. Oyster white. On one hung a dozen more Tyree Smiths. On another, Mexican tin masks. The back wall, except where a door broke it, was floor-to-ceiling shelves of shiny new art books, some of them turned to show their front covers. One was the history of Mexican art he'd seen in Ben Orton's study. The open floorspace was carpeted in oyster white. Big terra-cotta pre-Columbian figures squatted on top of plywood pedestals wrapped in monk's cloth. Spotlit. He didn't see any glass counter of art supplies, only a new desk where no one sat. The door in the bookshelf wall opened and a man came out.

He carried a splintered pine board that looked like part of a crate. A jimmy was in his other hand. Wisps of straw clung to his beard. Dave knew art-gallery types and this man wasn't one of them. He was strong and hard and his skin wasn't beach-tanned, it was tanned like leather. His beard might or might not ever have been trimmed. A twisted and knotted bandanna kept his long hair back. He wore a flimsy cotton shirt not made in U.S.A. and jeans not faded by the manufacturer. He didn't speak. His brows, thick and black and straight above startling blue eyes, did the questioning.

Dave said, "Did you buy the stock too?"

"It's still here." He jerked his head. "In back."

"The shop at the waterfront is closed. I need a couple of tubes of paint and a brush."

"I don't know anything about it," the man said, but he went out and came back with cardboard cartons. He turned one over and paint tubes and little boxes of paint tubes rattled out on the desk. Out of the other he dumped paper-taped clumps of brushes. "Help yourself." He stood back against the bookshelves and began to make a cigarette out of a Zig-Zag paper and Bugler tobacco. His fingers were thick and the blackness under the nails suggested he worked with machinery. When Dave chose slim tubes of black and white and a small sable brush, he said, "No colors?"

"What do I owe you?" Dave asked.

The man didn't hear. He was staring into the patio where voices were raised. Dave turned. Three of the sunhatted widows crossed under the jacaranda tree, making for the handweaver's shop. The voices weren't theirs. They swung around to stare at a pair who had come to a halt just inside the patio. The man was frail and white haired and wore a linen suit yellow with age, and the woman was gypsy-dark, in beads, sandals, a granny dress, hair around her head in thick braids. The man leaned at her, shouting.

"So I signed a paper. We're supposed to be friends."

"Tyree, shut up, darling. There's nothing to say. The man wants the pictures. I sold him the pictures. You gave me that right." She walked off.

"Not for pennies, I didn't." He caught her, turned her. "I came back from the dead to paint those pictures. Two thousand dollars!" He laughed but there was a sob in it. "A baseball player gets more than that for taking a deep breath." She twisted in his hands. He wouldn't let go. "You promised me a show. Two years I waited. I lived on that promise."

"You lived on vodka." She jerked free and came for the gallery, the flat soles of the sandals slapping the tiles. He lunged after her. He looked unsteady but she refused to run and he caught her again only steps from the gallery door.

"Since you didn't notice," he snarled, "I wasn't happy sweeping the floor, swabbing the john, framing daubs for lady tourists." He saw the widows gaping and stuck out his tongue at them. "I have talent, remember?"

"I kept my promise." She tugged a hand loose and waved it at the window where the watercolors hung. "There's your show for anyone to see. Only no one cares, Tyree. Can't you get that through your head? No one is buying."

"Are you saying they're bad?" He looked as if she'd knocked the wind out of him. He let her go. His next words begged and had tears in them. "You don't mean that, Mona."

She rubbed her arms where he'd gripped them. She tried to be calm and kind. "I mean they're too good for this location. That's why I set up this lunch with Castouros. He can sell them. They'll hang in nice homes—Santa Barbara, Malibu, Beverly Hills. They'll be looked at and admired. Tyree, I was doing you a favor. What do you want from me?

46

It's been a long, long time since you had two thousand dollars in a lump."

"He'll get ten thousand, twenty. That greasy Greek queen. An interior decorator, for God's sake! Why? What talent has he got? Why should a nothing like that—"

The bearded man had walked to the gallery door. Now he left it and stood in front of the fragile old man. "Go sober up," he said.

Smith shrank a little but he didn't go. "Franklin. This is your doing. You and your Mexican monstrosities. Do you know what those represent? A religion that cut the hearts out of living men. But of course you know that. That would suit you, Al. Just your style. Where do you keep that boat of yours?" He glanced around as if to find it dry-docked in one of the empty shops. "I'd like to bore a hole in it."

"Go sleep it off," Franklin said. "You're heading back to Monterey, remember? Those barroom buddies you miss so much? You can't pull a trailer on the Coast Road drunk." The woman had already come into the gallery. Al Franklin followed and shut the door. Tyree Smith stood teetering for a minute, staring after them with unfocused eyes. Then he staggered off. "Sorry about that," Franklin said to Dave.

"I'd buy that one." Dave indicated a sketch of pitted sea rock stippled with lichen, where a crab shell lay bleaching in the sun.

"I'm sorry," the woman said. "They're all sold."

"That's how it sounded." Dave held out the little paint tubes and the brush. "How much for these?"

"Take them," she said, and went out the door in the bookshelf wall. Dave looked at Franklin. Franklin raised the thick eyebrows again. "She's the boss," he said.

Dave glanced at the terra-cottas apologetically. "I doubt

that I can afford to buy one of those to make it up to you."

Franklin shrugged. "Forget it," he said.

The motel was new and hung over the marina. He stood at the glass wall, drying off after a quick shower, and watched sunbrown kids with sunbleached hair topple off little catamarans and clamber aboard again. He hung the red, white, and blue towel up and combed his hair, laid his suitcase on a red, white, and blue bedspread, and took from the suitcase blue denims, which he kicked into. A star-spangled Styrofoam tub of ice cubes had arrived while he showered. He dropped cubes into a clear plastic glass, dug a fifth of Old Crow from the suitcase, and made himself a stiff drink. He lit a cigarette, sat on the bed, and dialed a red, white, and blue telephone. While he waited for the desk nurse to fetch Amanda, he took two long swallows from the glass.

"He's the same," she said. "The doctor says that's good. It could turn around, Dave. It could."

"Hold the thought," he said. She was very young. He told her where to reach him, reading the number off the dial plaque. "It looks as if I'll be here a while. The situation is extremely phony. Unless you need me. It will be just as phony when I get back to it."

"Call tonight?" she said and sounded lonesome.

"I'd planned on around six," he said.

"Maybe he can talk to you then," she said. "If he's conscious, he'll want to talk to you."

"I'll want to talk to him," Dave said.

After he'd hung up, he dug the brush and tubes of paint from the jacket of his sweated suit. He slipped from the brown envelope marked KSDC-TV the photo of Ben Orton and laid it on the stingy motel-room desk. He filled another

48

plastic glass with water and sat at the desk to work on the photo, to change Ben Orton's image, give it a curly long-hair look under the slouch-brim leather hat, put mirror goggles on it, paint out the necktie and open the collar. The desk top was white Formica. He mixed his shades of gray on it. When he'd finished, it wiped off easily. He dropped brush and paints into the drawer. He let the photo lie on the desk to dry. And he used the phone again.

"Pets," Doug Sawyer's voice said. He was the neat, gray-haired man Dave lived with in big, awkward, sunny rooms above Doug's new art gallery on Robertson. But today, as for many days past, he was at his mother's shop in a gritty, run-down corner of Los Angeles between a bicycle store and a beauty shop. He was selling off the stock to other dealers. Food, bags of kibble, bins of birdseed. Fixtures—cages, fish tanks, counters, racks, refrigerators. While his plump, beaky little mother sat blankly, hands in lap, in the small house in back of the shop where Doug had grown up. Her mind was failing. It was a blood-circulation problem medicine couldn't do anything about. She'd tried to keep going with the shop, but animals, birds, fish were nothing you could be absentminded about. Or crazy. Doug had his own business to run, but unless he checked on her every day, food and water might not be supplied to the cages. Small lives could go out like matches in a wind. It was far to travel—Los Angeles is wide. And now she'd begun to neglect herself—forgetting to eat, to wash, to go to bed. Twice she'd lost her way on little trips to the supermarket and to the bank. Police had brought her home. On lucid days she tried to be cheerful, but it had begun to frighten her. It had frightened Doug for quite a while.

"Are you all right?" Dave asked.

"She set bacon grease on fire this morning," Doug said.

49

"If I hadn't got here when I did, the house would have burned. It's ninety-four degrees in L.A. and people aren't keeping appointments, and tomorrow I'll be tied up getting her into the rest home. Where are you?"

Dave told him and read him the phone number.

"What does it look like? Will you be gone forever?"

"Not if a lady keeps lying who has no talent for it," Dave said. "I saw some pre-Columbian pieces today that would make you drool."

"You're joking. Where? They're impossible to get, you know that. Since the Mexican government cracked down."

"Little gallery here. Big ones. Beauties."

"You're sure? For sale? Not just on exhibit?"

"I didn't ask. I'll check if I have time."

"Sure you will," Doug said. "How's your father?" And when Dave told him, he asked, "Do you want me to go to the hospital?"

"If I were there, I'd take Amanda to dinner," Dave said. "But you've got enough problems."

"Yours you can run away from," Doug said.

"I can't help him," Dave said. "Look—I asked you this morning—did you want me to stay?"

"Forget it," Doug said. "It's nerves, it's the heat."

"I'm better off working," Dave said. "That's all."

"Work, already," Doug said, and hung up.

Dave pushed his feet into rope-soled shoes and pulled over his head a denim tunic with white rope laces. He locked the numbered door and carried the photo in its envelope along the deck and down to street level. The silver Electra waited in its numbered slot beneath the building with a half-dozen other cars, but it sat too low. He frowned at the tires. Flat. He stepped to the other side of the car.

Again flat. He crouched and ran a hand over the near one. Slashed.

He stood, turned. Youths passed in baggy, flowered trunks, portering surfboards on their heads. A fat man in a cloth hat led a small girl by the hand. Both of them licked ice-cream cones. Sun flared off cars crowding the curbs. Across the street, one car had a police badge painted on its door. Raising a hand, Dave started for it. And it pulled out. Fast, tires shrieking. In five seconds, it had skidded out of sight around a corner. But Dave's mind kept a picture. Under his badged cap and dark glasses, the driver had been grinning. Straight at him.

7

The rental car was small. Each crack in the street jarred his spine. He left the bayfront, looking for and finding side streets of stingy stucco cottages, long unpainted, of dying trees sheltering rusty house trailers deep in brown weeds; business streets of corrugated-iron sheds; shops that dealt in secondhand ship's tackle or secondhand clothes; a pawnshop; a shop whose doorway loudspeaker laced the sunny air with rock music and in whose dirty windows record albums curled and faded. Two-by-fours were nailed across the doors of the Keyhole Theatre Adult Movies and someone had thrown a rock through the white plastic of the marquee.

A leathery old woman in a green transparent sunvisor dragged a wire shopping cart filled with sandy soft-drink bottles. A youth with bushy red hair sat with his back against a grapestake fence that enclosed a shrubby green nursery. He was playing a concertina. A girl in a granny dress slept with her head on his shoulder. Beside them leaned a sign in orange marker pen—BERKELEY. A weather-beaten man in a grimy yachting cap clutched a bottle in a paper sack at a round cement table beside a shiny glass-and-Formica hamburger stand that made the neighborhood look even sadder.

In a corner lot across from it, ribbed boat hulls hove up on warping scaffolds. Beyond them, smoke had blackened a storefront. Plywood with spray-can graffiti had been nailed over the window holes. Above them, a smoked and blistered sign read UNDERWATER PRESS. Next door, ging-ham cottage curtains hung behind a window lettered NATU-RAL FOODS CAFE & BAKERY. The little car made a U-turn with a briskness that surprised him. He parked it in front of the café.

A spring bell jingled when he opened the door. Flowers drawn in colored chalk brightened the walls. There was a good smell of baking. On the gingham-patterned Formica of the square tables lay soiled dishes. Lunch must have been a busy time. Bread was heaped inside an old-fashioned glass showcase at the back of the room. Through the doorway beyond it came a fresh-faced blond girl wrapped in a big white apron. She looked as merry as the chalked flowers. She seemed cheered to see him.

"Can I help you?"

"What's your best bread?" he asked.

"The seven-grain's great. Sprouted wheat—that's like you never tasted. I mean. And our best seller's carrot bread. See? The orange-colored ones."

"I'll have one of those," Dave said, and when she rattled open the slide door and took out the loaf and turned to drop it into a sack, he slipped the picture out of its envelope and laid it on the coin-scratched green glass of the counter top.

53

When she saw it the merriment went out of her. She frowned at the picture, frowned at him. He asked, "Ever see that man? Say a week ago Saturday?"

"Why?" She turned her head, watched him from the corners of her eyes. "Who are you?"

He laid his business card beside the picture. She read it without touching it. It didn't make her smile. Dave said, "He had life insurance with us. I need to know who he saw, what he was doing the day he died. He did come in here, didn't he?"

"He came in." A young male with a shaved head and little blue wire-frame glasses stood next to the girl. "He was asking questions. Did we know Lester Green. Did we know where Lester Green was."

The girl giggled. "Now you come asking do we know who he was—the man in the picture. And then somebody will come asking about you."

Dave glanced at the window. No police car showed itself on the sun-sad street, but he said, "It's possible," because it was. He asked blue glasses, "Did he tell you who he was?"

"He didn't want anybody to know. He wore a wig. He wore those mirror shades you can't see through."

The girl smiled wryly. "Hippie threads."

"He doesn't know there aren't any hippies anymore," the boy said. "He showed me grass. In a plastic folder. Pouch. Must've been six, eight ounces, maybe more. He said to pass the word to my customers—he'd give it all to whoever led him to Lester Green."

"To Lester Green for what?" Dave wondered.

"The bread's a dollar and a half, please," the girl said. Dave paid her. She rang the cash register and went into the back. A record began to play quietly from speakers hung in corners. Guitar, a sweet, simple soprano—"You can hear the boats go by, you can spend the night forever . . ." Ten years ago, wasn't it? These kids would have been in grammar school. What did it mean to them? Only that there were no hippies anymore?

"He said he'd heard Lester was out of jail." Blue glasses brought a yellow molded-plastic bin from behind the counter and began to dump into it the soiled plates and glasses from the tables. "He said Lester used to have good Mexican connections. Laughable."

"With dealers in marijuana?"

"Lester wouldn't go near it or anybody that had it on them if he knew they had it. He was very righteous."

"But he came in here?" Dave cocked an eyebrow.

"He wouldn't have. Somebody brought him."

"What did this man call himself?" Dave asked.

" 'Doc,' but that wasn't his name."

"No," Dave said. "Do you know his name?"

The bin was loaded. The boy carried it, jolting and clinking, into the back, saying over his shoulder, "Don't you?" Water began to splash hard in what sounded like a metal tub. There was a dusty smell of soap powder. The girl sneezed. Blue glasses came out with the empty bin.

Dave said, "So you didn't do what he wanted."

"Be serious." The boy was at the front tables now and his voice came back hardened and flattened from the window glass. "I could get what Lester got." A fork hit the floor and skittered away. He retrieved it. "Wow. It's hard to get used to. How different life around here is going to be without Ben Orton."

"There's his son," Dave said.

Blue glasses snorted. "Without his old man to tell him, he won't wipe his ass." He blinked at Dave. "I wonder what it feels like. Having everybody scared to death of you?"

55

"Except Anita?" Dave said.

"Yeah, well, Anita." The boy dumped more dishes into the bin, frowning to himself. "She wasn't exactly bright, either. Thought she could get away with anything. It didn't cost her. It cost Lester. And other people. Let me show you something." He left the bin on a table and opened the jingle-bell door. He went out into the sunlight. Dave followed. The boy pointed at the smoke-blackened storefront next door. "That was La Caleta's counterculture paper. We needed it. Have you seen the La Caleta *Tide?* The Sangre de Cristo *Bulletin?* You'd think Harding was still president. Oh, we've got Daisy Flynn. She can be sarcastic sometimes. The rednecks and the golden-agers hate her. But she can't really say much. The silver-saddle bastards that own the station won't let her. When it first started, she wrote a column for *Underwater.*" He nodded at the smoked storefront. "About twice. They told her, give it up or lose your job. She gave it up."

"How long did the paper last?" Dave said.

"Not long. Maybe a year. Then it was going to print what happened to Lester Green. The real story. And that night the place burned up."

"So the story never came out?" Dave said.

"The guy was a paraplegic. Vietnam. Eddie Suchak. Hell, able-bodied people couldn't fight Orton. Eddie must have figured he was lucky not to have burned up with his press. He split. Never heard of him again till they had it on the news. Ten days, two weeks ago maybe. He died. Some VA hospital up in the Bay area."

"What was the real story?" Dave asked.

"All he told me was, he had documentary proof." Blue glasses went back into the café and began clearing the last tables while Dave watched. "He was in here for supper, like

56

always, and he said he'd gotten this Xerox. From Sacramento. Some state office. He was laughing and rubbing his hands, you know? He was going to wipe out Ben Orton with one column of print. Shit."

"Who did you tell?" Dave asked.

The boy swung around and stared at him. "What?"

"You don't think that fire was an accident. You think Ben Orton was back of it. You have steady customers. You talk freely to me. I expect you talk freely to them. Somebody had to tell Ben Orton. How else would he know?"

"Jesus," the boy whispered.

"That must have been quite a document," Dave said.

The boy looked sulky and went off with the bin of dirty dishes. When he came out, he said, "Nobody that hangs out here would go to Ben Orton. Ben Orton was feared, man. It made everybody very nervous when Anita started coming around all the time. When that car of hers would pull up at the curb, there'd be groans, you know? She was into revolution, right? Like a lot of rich kids. We didn't lay back till she went off to join Cesar Chavez, the farm workers. Only it didn't last. Her old man dragged her home. Then she started coming in with Lester."

"Did that relax anyone?" Dave asked.

"Like something ticking in a briefcase. By luck, it didn't go off here. It went off when they stopped Lester's Kawasaki and untaped that lid of grass from under the fender."

"Did she come back after that?"

"What do you think?"

"I think La Caleta is a small town," Dave said, "and Sangre de Cristo isn't that far off and isn't that much bigger. Ben Orton had to know his daughter was going with a black

57

boy. What suddenly made him interfere? What was it your editor friend next door had?"

"You want me to guess?" blue glasses asked.

"I don't see how you can miss," Dave said.

The boy drew a breath. "Marriage license," he said. "But nobody gets married anymore. That's crazy."

"That's why it fits so well," Dave said.

Inside the grapestake fence, the humidity climbed. Long ribbons of flat green plastic, shiny as new snakes, hung in lazy swags across redwood beams and dripped water on boxed trees and shrubs below. The smell of earth was thick. Farther on, high yardages of cheesecloth bellied white above flats of seedlings. In a wide gravel square, cacti soaked up sun. In a wheelbarrow, cropped rose canes stuck thornily out of burlap-bundled root clumps.

Dave came to a neat, flat-roofed shed building with big new front windows. Planter boxes, fresh and empty, were piled around it, big heavy terra-cotta pots, glazed pots, garden figurines. Inside, canaries sang among hanging ferns. Shelves held bottled plant food and insect killer, bright colored watering cans, bundles of cotton gardening gloves. New trowels, rakes, hoes hung against the wooden walls. Sacked potting soil and fertilizer banked a counter. But nobody tended the store.

The acre grew jungly toward the back. He passed a battered pickup truck without side window-glass and found, almost hidden by bamboo that rustled high and sunlit in a breeze he couldn't feel, a shingle-sided cottage with deep eaves and a low porch. The door stood open and inside a slim brown kid in ragged shorts lay on his stomach on the floor using a telephone. Beyond him, a silent color television set showed tear-glossy soap-opera faces. It was a big set and looked new.

"That is the most fucked-up way to run a business I ever heard of," ragged shorts said, and slammed down the receiver. He rolled over and sat up. He was one of those pretty boys who grow old fast. His skin was toughening. His jaw hinges were developing knobs. His eyes had begun to back off under too much brow ridge. They saw Dave. "What's the matter?" he said.

"Does something have to be the matter?" Dave asked.

"Around here it does." He stood up. "You want some help? See the old man."

"The old man is across the street at Jack in the Box, drinking Thunderbird out of a paper sack," Dave said.

Ragged shorts muttered, *"Cabrón."*

"There aren't any customers," Dave said. "I didn't come to buy. I came to talk to Hector Rodriguez."

Light flickered in the shadowed eyes. "What about?"

"Cliff Kerlee. Why he's in jail. Are you Rodriguez?"

"Who wants to know?" He had work-hardened hands. They made fists like clubs. Dave told him who he was. The fists relaxed. With an amazed shake of his head and a sad laugh, he left off blocking the door. "Come in. Man, you are a hard man to find, you know?" He bent for the phone and set it on a low white wrought-iron table whose glass top was strewn with gaudy seed catalogues. "Come in, sit down, Mr. Brandstetter." There was a beanbag chair. There were two chairs of green canvas slung in iron frames. With the table and television set, they were all the furniture there was. Against a wall where two strips of flocked crimson paper had been pasted up lay a big roll of carpet that looked new. Unopened gallon cans of paint waited beside it. In the center of a ceiling where cracks had lately been patched, a bright little crystal chandelier tinkled in the same impalpable breeze that moved the bamboo. Rodriguez switched off the television set. *"Hay mucho calor,"* he said. "Hot. Will you join me in a beer?"

"Sounds good, thanks." Dave sat in one of the sling chairs. Rodriguez went through an empty dining room where a built-in sideboard had diamond-shaped glass panes. He pushed out of sight through lumberyard-bargain louver doors that hadn't been painted. Dave called after him, "It had to be television. You heard about me on the news—right?"

"I telephoned Channel Ten." Rodriguez appeared with sweaty brown bottles and slender glasses with too much gold filigree. "Soon as I could. People came, and the old man is no use. It was perhaps half an hour. You had been there but you had gone." He handed Dave one of the flossy glasses and filled it. The beer was dark, the label Mexican. He set the bottle on the floor by Dave's chair and folded into the beanbag chair and filled his own glass. He said, "I telephoned your company in Los Angeles. It was a hassle getting the number from the operator and all that. You dial and dial. And then"—he drank from his glass and wiped his mouth with the back of a hand—"they didn't know where you were. They said they would call me back. That's why I am here." He gestured with the glass. "Out there is much work to do. Without Cliff, twice as much. But I waited here for them to call. And they did. Just now. They still don't know where you are."

"I'm not sure, myself," Dave said. The taste of the beer was dark as its color. "What did you want me for?"

"You don't think Cliff killed him." Rodriguez had to stretch to reach cigarettes on the table. He tossed the pack to Dave. "I know Cliff didn't kill him."

"He was here with you, right?" They were Mexican cigarettes. The paper was brown. Dave took one and tossed back the pack. "Never left the place all day?"

"We were trying to fix up this house." Rodriguez lit a cigarette with a paper match. "We done quite a bit at nights. But you get tired, you know? When we got this nursery nobody had had it for a long time. It took a lot of work to get it nice again so people would come. For many weeks we slept in sleeping bags on the floor in here."

Dave grinned. "Under a crystal chandelier."

"That is what you call the gay life-style," Rodriguez said, but his smile didn't amount to much. "It didn't matter. We were at peace. For a while."

"What happened to it?" Dave used the steel lighter on his cigarette. The sweet taste of the smoke took him back to boyhood trips down Baja with his father. In lost, sun-cracked *cantinas* behind dusty gas pumps, the unshaven barkeeps would sell cigarettes to kids. He used to hoard them in his blanket roll to smuggle home. He looked at his watch—not for *la hora de cenar,* when he could talk to Ophelia Green, but for six o'clock, when he could call the hospital again. It would be a while yet. "I saw the city-hall demonstration on film today. Your friend Kerlee didn't look peaceable."

"He hates injustice," Rodriguez said. "It makes him crazy. I told him to stay out of it. Why we came up here from L.A. was to leave all that activist shit behind. Ten years was enough. It never did no good. It only made him old. And poor. He gave it all his time, every penny he could get. Phone ringing at two in the morning. There's always some flit in trouble. There always will be till the straights change, and you can't change them. I told Cliff, they got to hate somebody. What have they got? Fat-ass wives that whine all the time, bills and payments, kids that turn out to be junkies and whores and car thieves. They got to think somebody is more miserable than they are. Or happier. That's worse. Gays can't do nothing right. Come out or hide—it don't change nothing. They'll always hate us. Or envy us. Or pity us. Take your choice."

"Every penny from where?" Dave asked.

"*Qué?* Oh—a boutique. Potted plants. Near a big hospital, so it did good. But if I didn't hide half what we took in—put it in a separate bank Cliff didn't know nothing about—we'd have been out on our *nalgas*. Then I heard about this place—for sale cheap because it was run down. I drove up. Last July, weekend of the parade. It looked great to me. I told Cliff, 'Either we take it or it's over between us.'" Gloomily Rodriguez dumped the rest of the beer from his bottle into the fancy glass. "So, it's all my fault. I should never have—"

"It's someone else's fault," Dave said. "What parade?"

"You know, man. Gay Pride Week? Every year. To celebrate 1969 when those drag queens threw their purses at the New York police. Cliff was always in that parade up to his *ano*. But why celebrate drag queens? They spend their whole life celebrating. They don't do nothing but make the rest of us look bad." Rodriguez shook his head and smiled scornfully. "Gay pride! What does that mean, man?"

"Two strips of flocked wallpaper?" Dave said.

"Yeah. Shit." Surprisingly, Rodriguez started to laugh. "He had the bucket of paste. The paper was rolled out on the floor facedown. He was on his knees, brushing paste on the back when they came in. No knock, no nothing. Three big ones. He jumped up and said what is this or something. And they said he killed Ben Orton, and Cliff slopped the brush in the paste and painted the first cop. Right from the top down." Rodriguez wiped his eyes. "Wow, that cop looked funny. Like some old movie, you know? One big, long stroke of the brush."

"Getting on their good side from the start," Dave said.

"Man, there is no way to get on their good side." Left-over laughter jerked the smooth brown chest, made the shoulders jump. Rodriguez hiccuped but he meant what he said and he said it grimly. "I told them he was here all day with me. Told them and told them. They don't care."

"You're going to have to tell them something better."

"I did. They don't care about that neither. The district attorney—he don't care about it. Even dead, this is still Ben Orton's town. Everyone is in his pocket. Judges too. You don't think Cliff can get a fair trial, do you?" Mouth clamped in bitterness, Rodriguez reached to twist out his cigarette in an abalone-shell ashtray on the table. "Daisy Flynn knew Cliff, interviewed him twice on TV. I told her. She don't care, neither. *Puta.*"

"Told her what?" Dave got out of the canvas chair to use the ashtray. "That you know who killed Orton?"

"Why do you care?" Rodriguez asked suddenly.

"It's a matter of seventy-five thousand dollars."

"Money." Rodriguez looked pained. "Don't you care about justice? Don't you care about Cliff?"

"I care that he didn't kill Ben Orton. I care that he was set up for it. I'd care to know who set him up because the odds are good that if I knew that I'd know who killed Ben Orton. If it was his wife or his son, I'd care deeply. Was it his wife or his son?"

"It was Richard T. Nowell," Rodriguez said.

8

Richard T. Nowell said, "They get overexcited." The hand-loomed jacket he'd worn in that snatch of film Dave had seen at KSDC-TV hung in some closet now. He had on only swim trunks. His spare, tanned body didn't show his age. Neither did his hair, which had been to that high-priced barber again. It was gray but it grew thick and healthy. What showed his age were his eyes, hard, bright, and wary —eyes that had seen too much and doubted most of it. "Hispanos—as alike as jumping beans. There is no reality, only romance. Cervantes knew it in 1605. Nothing's changed."

He lay with a silvery drink in his hand on a chaise of aluminum tubing and bright yellow flowered fabric on a *terraza* in back of a hillside house like Ben Orton's—rough white stucco, grilled windows, red-tile roofs. It looked as if repair work was underway on the roofs. Stacks of new tiles occupied a corner of the *terraza,* along with trowels, buckets, ladders. An ornamental iron gate opened into the property from above. There was a tennis court where youths in shorts batted a yellow ball over a green net. Long stairs led down here. Another long flight dropped to a blue pool where young men laughed and splashed. Below the pool, a brushy fold in the fall-off of land put the highway out of sight. Beyond lay the small roofs of La Caleta, the bay with its tiny white boats, the rusty jut of the old cannery, the sparkling ocean.

Dave said, "He told me you and Kerlee were enemies. Hated each other's guts. Always had."

"Cliff didn't need enemies," Nowell said. "He had himself." A blond youth with long, smooth swimmer's muscles came out French doors onto the terrace. Maybe his trunks weren't as small as possible but they looked it. Nowell fluttered fingers at him. "Get Mr. Brandstetter a drink, will you?" He looked at Dave. "What shall it be?"

"It has been Mexican beer." Dave smiled at the youth. That was easy. "Whatever's in the fridge."

The boy smiled back, said "Löwenbräu" firmly, and took Nowell's empty glass into the house.

"Winning child," Nowell said, looking after him. "He was slated for the Olympics. Did nothing but train. From the age of eight. Isn't it insane? His father says he'd have made the team. But there were locker-room problems."

"Come to you in trouble, do they?" Dave asked.

"By referral. Doctors, lawyers, agencies, juvenile authorities. Even the odd police department."

Dave blinked. At the noisy pool below, at the *plock* of balls on rackets above. "All of them?"

"No, no." Nowell shook his head, amused. "These are

mostly just neighbor children come to play. You know how it is when you have a pool."

Dave grinned. "Awful nuisance."

"Hateful." Nowell's hard eyes twinkled. "No, the counseling's handled down at the office. Now and then I have a case who lives here. There's plenty of room. Boys. Girls. And parents, of course."

As if on cue, a stocky man with a mat of gray hair on a sagging chest came around a corner of the house. He wore floppy surfer trunks, a loud Hawaiian shirt, and clogs. He carried towels. He was bald and his sunburned scalp was peeling. A woman followed him. She was burned too dark and had starved herself to keep her figure right for a bikini and had almost managed it. The smiles these people gave Nowell showed astonishing teeth. The man had to be a dentist. Self-conscious, they nudged each other down toward the hectic pool.

"Do they pay?" Dave said.

"We're a nonprofit educational—"

"You always were," Dave said, "only I remember you in a pair of dingy offices around Third and Main in L.A. Building about to be torn down?"

Nowell laughed. "We used to beat pans and shriek in the hall," he said, "to warn the rats we were coming. It was nice to have them out but they never tidied up before they left. Yes, those were the bad old days. A secondhand mimeograph, three frightened faggots, and a cause. Twenty-five years ago. You came there?"

"You were *amicus curiae* in the case of a friend of a friend. He didn't have a car. I did. I picked him up at your place one day in the rain. We shook hands but I don't expect you to remember. You must have been *amicus curiae*

66

to a good many bewildered schoolteachers plucked naked out of steam baths."

"We were in court more hours than we slept."

"You had a magazine too," Dave said. "Don't I remember an obscenity case?"

"Poor, pathetic little rag," Nowell said. "By today's standards it was tame as a Sunday-school paper. But it helped. It told thousands of sad, lonely boys and men all over this country that they weren't the only ones. You should have seen the letters, the pitiful dollar bills. Yes, there was an obscenity case. We fought it. We fought the police, the civil service, the armed forces. There was so much to fight. There still is."

"But you quit," Dave said. "Why?"

"Quit?" Nowell said sharply. "Who says I quit?"

"Besides Rodriguez," Dave said, "Daisy Flynn, and Ben Orton's widow. But mostly"—Dave looked at the place—"all this." The swimmer brought back his tightly packaged genitals, his smile, and the drinks. He went whooping down the stairs toward the pool. Dave said, "This didn't come out of pitiful dollar bills."

"They were never enough," Nowell said. "It was my own money that kept us going. You should have seen how I had to live. A quarter century of cockroaches, crackers, and peanut butter. It wasn't only court costs. Men were fired, boys were thrown out at home. People tried to kill themselves, mutilate themselves. They needed doctors, psychiatrists, jobs, a roof over their heads."

"Those two A.M. phone calls," Dave said.

"Someone had to answer. Someone had to come up with the money."

Dave looked at the house. "From here?"

Nowell snorted. "Least of all. My father made Ben Orton

look like a left-wing radical. You can imagine the rejoicing when his only son turned out to be a bird of bright plumage. The festivities went on for months. I cherish his parting words—that looking at me made him want to vomit."

Dave's father said, "You're full of surprises."

Dave said, "I kept waiting for you to guess."

"No," Nowell said, "I had a little annuity from a great aunt. Then, four years ago, five"—with a crooked smile he tried his drink—"my father died. Happily, he was the self-made type, tall in the saddle, short in the brain. He distrusted Jew shysters—his pet term for lawyers. Ergo, he made such an incompetent will that I ended up with this house he never wanted me to set foot in, and all his money." The smile went away. "What did Daisy Flynn say to make you think I'd quit? I'd never quit."

"I saw her introduction to a TV interview." Dave tasted the German beer. American refrigeration had numbed it. "You and Kerlee. On the matter of Ben Orton's refusal to hire homosexuals. She said the two of you disagreed. I knew how Kerlee felt. How you felt had to follow."

"If you'd seen the interview—" A striped beach ball, shedding bright water, flew over the balustrade. Nowell had quick reflexes. He hit it with the flat of a hand. It arced high and dropped. Cheers came from below. "—You'd have heard Cliff raving on about getting up petitions, showing that the citizens of La Caleta wanted fruity cops even if their police chief didn't. It was an insane idea, like every other idea Cliff Kerlee ever had."

"He got the signatures," Dave said. "How?"

"You'd never guess it to look at him," Nowell said, "but he's a great charmer of women. The gypsy syndrome or something. Those wild eyes. You can bet nine-tenths of those signatures were written in dishwashing liquid. Can't you just see the poor things in their curlers and damp blue jeans blushing and stammering and scorching the TV dinners while that hypersexed aging adolescent lounged in the kitchen doorway looking sullen and rubbing his crotch?"

"You're forgetting why he was there," Dave said. "They'd have to know he was bent."

"Women never believe that," Nowell scoffed. "Each of them harbors a secret conviction that men are only homosexual because they haven't met the right woman—herself, of course. Cliff knows that and he uses it."

"It didn't help," Dave said. "Ben Orton wasn't wearing curlers."

"I warned Cliff." Nowell watched Dave hunch over the steel lighter to start a cigarette in the sea wind. "On that interview. And later."

"So Rodriguez says." Smoke from the cigarette blew away thin and quickly. Dave pocketed the lighter. "You were there Saturday morning. Early. Telling him to cancel the demonstration. Rodriguez says you grabbed the petitions to tear them up. There was a fight. You rolled around together on the floor."

Nowell showed neat, feral little teeth. "I wasn't hurt. I'm not big but I'm wiry."

"You're also over forty," Dave said.

Nowell shrugged. "It's not my way of solving problems. It's Cliff's. But he's not built for it and he's not prepared. I was a commando in the U.S. Army. If Rodriguez hadn't been there, his friend would have gone to the hospital."

"But you don't hate him," Dave said dryly.

A tall, fleshy young man in a red chef's hat and a red chef's apron came fussily onto the terrace, wheeling a round, red enamel barbecue outfit. "Yawl gonna be ready to eat in an hour?" he asked the air. He had a loud voice but Nowell acted as if he hadn't heard. A yellow and black sack of charcoal leaned against a stack of tiles. The aproned man picked it up. "They ever gonna finish this roof?" Maybe he didn't expect an answer, because he made a lot of noise emptying briquettes into the belly of the grill. "Did yawl call 'em?"

"Shut up, Harv," Nowell said without turning.

"Dick, I told you I'd call 'em." Harv moved with wiggles and flounces. He set the sack back in place. "All you have to do is say for me to call 'em and I'll call 'em." He poured lighter fluid from a flat can onto the coals. "I declare, with all this junk piled up here, there's just no room for a person to move."

"Harv, shut up," Nowell said again.

"How is a person supposed to cook?" Harv bent and took from under the barbecue a cardboard tube printed with kitcheny flowers. A long match came out of this. "If yawl didn't get your ribs or steaks or chicken on the dot at six" —he struck the match, stood well back, turned away his face, and poked the flame at the coals; the lighter fluid whooshed—"it'd be me yawl would bitch at. Dick, are you listenin' to me?"

"I'll call them tomorrow," Nowell said. "Now shut up, will you?"

"Yawl say that every night." Harv flapped at the coals with his apron. Smoke swirled up. "Now, if yawl don't remember tomorrow, I declare I'm just gonna call 'em myself, that's all."

"If you call them, you'll quarrel with them, and they'll never come back."

"Well, just look here what they did. Spilled all that wet mortar. Dribbles of it all along here. Hard as a rock. Look how ugly that looks." He coughed in the smoke. "Who's

70

gonna clean that up? Not me. I've got plenty to do around here already." He fitted a grill over the coals. "And look how they stacked these tiles. They are topplin' over, Dick." He bumped one of the stacks hard with a well-padded hip. "One of these days, one of 'em is gonna slip right off. They are heavy. If one of 'em falls on somebody down there, it could kill 'em."

"If it falls on that side, it can only kill a ground squirrel," Nowell said. "Now, as you can see, I have a guest, and I'd appreciate it if you'd shut up."

"I'll get the steaks." Harv went away.

Nowell acted as if there'd been no interruption. He said to Dave, "No, I didn't hate him. You don't hate a madman. You try to keep him from hurting himself. I went to the nursery that morning to try and stop him making a laughingstock of himself and every other homosexual that walks. That demonstration was going to drop his chances of getting what he wanted to zero."

"Where did his troops come from?" Dave asked. "They didn't look like they belonged here."

"From L.A.—the seedier bars, the slimier baths."

"Had he phoned them? Would Rodriguez let him?"

"He wouldn't have to. Not if that press conference of Orton's was on television." Nowell raised his head. Gulls came over the high red roof, wings creaking, straining into the onshore wind, headed for the beach. "They'd see it as only one thing, the chance for a demonstration—noise, obscene gestures, dirty words on signs. If possible, riot and arrest. Maybe with luck a bloody head. Never accomplishes anything. That's why they love it. Another chance at defeat. And, of course, their leader was here."

"Why was he here?" Dave asked. "I mean, Rodriguez

71

told me his reason for getting Cliff out of L.A. You'd left those two A.M. phone calls for him to answer all alone."

Nowell made a small, sour sound. "And God help the poor callers. They didn't know what trouble was before they picked up that phone. He could double it for them by noon. Listen to me. I never stopped answering. I certainly did not leave everything to him."

"They stopped calling you," Dave said.

"Exactly. In our mousy little office with our mousy little magazine, minding our business, getting things done. Then, all of a sudden, here came the clowns. Calliopes, elephants, performing seals. The television people went mad. Naturally. I mean, anyone making a total ass of himself is bound to raise ratings. And everybody always knew homosexuals were a bunch of overgrown little girls painting their faces and getting themselves up in mommy's best organdy. What more could the media ask for? Never a five-minute serious discussion. But screaming queens? Ha ha! Isn't it killing?"

"It made them easy to find," Dave said.

"Do yawl know"—Harv came bustling out, carrying a metal tray heaped with steaks—"what the two main floats were in that first parade down Hollywood Boulevard?" He set the tray on a Formica-top table with fold-down aluminum tube legs. "A crucified fairy with jeweled purple wings, and a ten-foot-high jar of Vaseline. What every bigot knew about homosexuality and never needed to ask."

Nowell answered Dave, "It made us impossible to find."

Steaks hit the grill and sizzled. In his red apron Harv went at a wiggle to lean over the balustrade. He waved a long-handled fork and shouted down at the pool. "Yawl better get your showers because it is supper time." The wind took off his chef's hat. He was bald under it. With a yelp, he chased it across the *terraza*.

72

"I'll go," Dave said, and stood.

Harv was on hands and knees in a far corner. Only his broad, blue-denimed butt, the red bow of the apron, the white soles of his Adidas showed. But his hearing was good. "Yawl are welcome to stay." His voice came muffled. "Fresh corn on the cob? Genuine Mississippi beaten biscuits?" He pulled the hat from behind the stacks of tiles, sat back on his heels, slapped dust off the hat. "Homemade Texas pecan pie?"

"Sounds great," Dave said, "but I have an appointment."

"Go fetch him." Harv stood up and settled the puffy red hat on his dome. "Bring him back. He's welcome."

"It's not that kind of appointment," Dave said, and to Nowell, "Didn't they sort of make it easier for you? To get on with what you were doing? Fewer interruptions?"

"What really needed doing," Nowell said, "wasn't parades and picket lines and protests. It was changing the laws. For twenty years we tried single-handed. Now and then some new assemblyman still wet from the egg would flutter into the lion's den with a timid little bill. They always ate him." Nowell sighed and pushed up from the chaise. "Then, at long last, we got an experienced man on our side." He moved his mock teenager's body to the top of the stairs. "Someone who could do it right, who had the necessary committee chairmanships, the necessary power."

"And you got the laws changed," Dave said.

"We did not." Nowell leaned out to peer down at the pool. "Come on, you tragic misfits." He turned back to Dave. "Not then. We rounded up twenty expert witnesses, psychiatrists, law professors, police chiefs—"

"Not Ben Orton," Dave said.

Nowell gave him a pitying look and went on. "We sat at long hearing-room tables being glared at by bleary-eyed political hacks who went after us, day after day, with questions like dull castration knives. Then we waited."

The boys from the pool came scrambling up the stairs, water streaming from long, wet-dog hair and laying a glaze on uncompleted bodies. They waved towels like guidons. A couple of them brushed Nowell's sunken cheek with kisses before they followed the rest, laughing, shouting, dodging, into the house.

Nowell's neat little teeth smiled after them a moment. Then he saw Dave again and went back to his story. "Finally a phone call came from Sacramento. Our friend had lined up the votes. A slim majority, but enough." His mouth twisted. "Unless you remembered Cliff Kerlee."

"What did he have to do with it?"

A hefty girl with flushed cheeks and chopped blond hair came out the French doors. She wore tight, faded jeans over bulging hips. Her short-sleeved sweat shirt was stenciled OAKLAND RAIDERS. She pushed a stainless-steel restaurant cart on wheels. The shelves were loaded with plates, cutlery, napkins, drinking glasses. A girl who could have been her twin followed, hands in padded oven mittens, lugging a boiler that steamed. When she set it down and Harv removed the lid, Dave saw bobbing ears of corn. Harv poked at them and put back the lid.

Nowell said, "He took his troops, as you call them, to the capital. And when the vote came up, they rushed screaming onto the floor, trailing chiffon scarves and clouds of dime-store perfume, and hugging and kissing every legislator they could catch." Nowell tilted up his glass, tilted back his head, rattled ice against his mouth. "We didn't get the vote."

"Someone got it," Dave said. "Consenting adults?"

"Years later. And it wasn't me." Nowell sounded bitter. "A lifetime of work. For nothing. Nothing."

"Which makes it a little hard to understand," Dave said, "how Kerlee ended up here. La Caleta isn't that big or that popular. Finding the two of you—"

"My folks live in L.A.," Harv said. "I go there all the time." He was spearing steaks and flopping them onto plates. He yelled at the house, "Somebody better come and eat these. I mean it." Laying new steaks on the grill while the football girls loaded corn and biscuits onto the plates, Harv told Dave above the sizzle, "Now Dick doesn't agree with me, but I believe that if somebody is gay, it doesn't matter if he is black or white or red all over, he is my brother. I don't care if he agrees about what we should do —I'm talkin' about politics now—we are on the same side. We can't help but be on the same side. We want the same things, don't we, after all?"

"Do we?" Nowell said. "Harv, you are a fool."

Harv paid him no attention. "And I also patronize gay businesses. It's my policy." He fanned smoke away from his face. "I wanted a piggyback plant for my sister's birthday. I went to Cliff Kerlee's shop."

"And took your mouth along," Nowell said.

"Don't interrupt now," Harv told him. But it was the dentist with the peeling scalp and the sun-mummified wife who interrupted. They toiled up the steps, crowing about the good smells. Harv bustled around them, unfolding tube-and-web chairs, laying napkins across their laps, fetching them heaped plates. That taken care of, Harv went back to the grill, forked over the steaks, and told Dave, "And little Rodriguez was saying how he wanted to get Cliff out of L.A. Well, yawl better believe it—I knew what he meant." Harv glared at Nowell.

"How you could even speak to him is beyond me," Nowell said. "After what Cliff Kerlee did to us."

"Dick, I am not vindictive like you." Harv tossed imaginary curls. "I cannot go on hatin' people. I certainly cannot go on hatin' my gay brothers."

"I may throw up," Nowell said.

Harv looked at Dave. "And I remembered that vacant nursery up here in La Caleta goin' to seed, dyin' for somebody to take it over, somebody with a green thumb."

"Lavender, you mean," Nowell said.

"Exactly. If I had my way, every business in this town would be gay. If yawl would stop hatin' and start lovin', this would be a better world. We have got to stick together, Dick. How many times have I told you that?"

"Eight hundred fifty-four thousand?" Nowell asked.

Harv told Dave, "And little Rodriguez drove up here and loved the place and that's how come Dick Nowell and Cliff Kerlee are both in the same little town. And I don't feel one tiny bit sorry."

"I expect," Dave said, "Kerlee feels sorry enough for both of you."

"Well, it's not my fault," Harv said. "Ben Orton started it. Dick Nowell's father figure. He talks about my big mouth. It was Ben Orton's big mouth that got Cliff Kerlee all stirred up." Harv turned. "Dodo? Angie? Bring plates. These are done."

Dodo and Angie brought plates. Boys in sweat suits came out the French doors. A boy in a brown and orange dashiki followed. So did a boy in a white terrycloth robe. They made loud vocal noises and plate-clattering noises. "Butter!" somebody said. "Parkay!" somebody else said. Chairs rattled, unfolding. A green toy balloon came out an upstairs window, a scrap of paper fluttering from it. The wind caught the balloon, rubbed it along the stucco to a high corner of the house, and carried it off across the scrubby hills. At the window, a boy in a striped tank top wailed, "Aw, that was my order for room service."

"Yawl would look lovely skewered on my rotisserie," Harv called. "You get on down here."

Dave said to Nowell, "Father figure?"

"Harv's never forgiven me." Nowell took Dave's arm and led him toward the stairs that climbed beside the house to the gate and road above. "After Ben Orton's foot-in-mouth TV appearance," Nowell said, "I had him and his wife up here to dinner."

"You startle me," Dave said.

"There was no way they could refuse. My family owned this town before the name Orton was ever heard of."

"Dinner?" Dave eyed the *terraza,* the jumping, joky boys, the napkins wrapped by the wind around their ankles, the suety smoke. "Here?"

"It wasn't like this." Nowell started up the stairs and Dave followed. "It was indoors, private, and very sedate. Silver candelabra. Vintage wine. Spanish-lace tablecloth." The shadow of the house turned the tennis court grape-juice color. The yellow ball lay there glowing. Nowell went and picked it up. "The best bourbon before. Chateaubriand. The best brandy afterward. Cuban cigars. Viennese coffee."

"Sounds persuasive," Dave said. "Did it work?"

Nowell grimaced. "It lacked a lovely woman."

"I've heard that about him," Dave said.

"Then you've talked to someone knowledgeable."

"Daisy Flynn," Dave said.

"She was one of the first." Unexpectedly, Nowell threw the ball. High. Onto the house roof. He stood waiting, face turned up, a thin, gray-haired kid. "A gay, laughing, red-headed colleen. Cub reporter on the Sangre de Cristo *Bulletin.*" The ball rolled down the tiles, bounced, did a dying fall into Nowell's hands. "My mother used to write me all the gossip."

"And somebody gossiped to Louise Orton, right?"

Nowell wandered to a green slat bench. "After that"— he found a can lying there, dropped the ball into it, fitted on the lid—"our Ben was careful to put geography between Louise and the other woman—women."

"How long did it go on?" Dave wondered.

"As long as he continued to breathe," Nowell said. "At least—Harv and I saw him at a corner table, very discreet, in a little restaurant we thought only we knew about. Nirvana, it's called. In the hills at Monterey. How long ago?" He squinted at the luminous sky. "Six weeks—eight? He was holding hands with a woman. No longer quite young but still handsome. Dark, brooding. Thick black braids, pottery beads, handmade sandals. I think she runs an art gallery. But then, who doesn't in Monterey?"

"Louise Orton wouldn't know about Nirvana?"

"I doubt she'd know anything a hundred-odd miles would let her avoid knowing. You should have seen her here that night. Smitten with him as a new bride."

"What you wanted from him was what Kerlee wanted."

"Said he wanted, but could never get," Nowell said. "He didn't understand men like Orton. I did, do. I grew up among them. Right here. Present them with a human problem any more complicated than hello or good-bye and they know only two things to do"—he started up the remaining dozen steps to the tall gate—"fuck it or stomp it. You don't force them. Not into anything. Certainly not anything fruity. Certainly not in public."

78

Dave followed him. "Is this what you said on that Daisy Flynn TV show?"

"In different words."

"Louise Orton told me you were a thorn in his side. At a guess, he could live with that. The evidence says he did. The porno movie closed. The underground paper. I didn't see a boarded-up massage parlor but there was one, wasn't there?"

"If you want to win a fight"—Nowell used the tight little smile again—"you choose issue, time, and place."

"Only you didn't win," Dave said. "Or did you?"

Nowell's hand was on the iron latch of the gate. He turned, frowning. "What does that mean?"

"Who were you fighting—Orton or Kerlee?"

"What exactly did Hector Rodriguez tell you?"

"That sometime after the riot, you sneaked back to the nursery and took Kerlee's leather bag out of the pickup. He didn't see you—he just knows that was how it had to be. You took the bag up to Orton's, smashed his head in, and left the bag beside the body to frame Kerlee."

"Now you listen to me," Nowell said. "Cliff Kerlee's entire life was a headlong rush at self-destruction. He was violent. There was only one way for it to end." Nowell swung open the gate. "And that's the way it ended."

Dave went out onto the dusty road. Something whirred in the hilltop brush. He wondered what kind of insect it was. He'd heard the same sound when he'd walked out of the nursery an hour ago. He looked. Nothing stirred in the long sundown shadows. "Where were you when it ended?"

"Where I always am at that hour," Nowell said. "In a favorite cove of mine up the beach. Meditating." His look was steady and mocking. "No, don't ask. Nobody saw me."

9

Tired plumbing made the flimsy house shudder. Behind her somewhere there was the hard tumble of water into a bathtub. She was tall bones inside a housecoat faded from many washings. Above high, broad cheekbones, her eyes tilted. Their whites were stained like old porcelain. Her hair was streaked with gray but he doubted she was fifty. She kept the screen door hooked between them.

"How could he be here? They sent him to prison two years ago. It was a mistake. Lester wouldn't do anything outside the law. Last thing he would touch is marijuana. Some other boy must have got the wrong motorcycle in the dark. Then the police stopped Lester."

"He's been out of prison since the sixteenth," Dave said. "His parole officer told me he was living here. Aren't those his clothes piled up on your washing machine?"

"Those are Bernard Stein's clothes," she said. "His mama and papa are on an Arctic cruise. I look after their house. Bernard didn't come to me with those till I was set to go home. I brought 'em along to wash up here for him."

"Lester owed you a lot," Dave said. "It doesn't seem right—his not coming straight home to you. At least he could have telephoned. He telephoned Anita Orton."

"I don't have a telephone," she said. "I can't afford it. Who is Anita Orton?"

"She drove him to his parole officer's," Dave said. "Then she drove him here, didn't she?"

"I don't know any Anita Orton," Ophelia Green said. "You'll have to go now. My tub will run over." She shut the wooden door with its neatly curtained cracked glass pane. The sagging boards of the stoop under his feet shook to her retreating steps. He raised knuckles to knock again, heard a car coming in low gear up the steep road, and turned. Through drooping pepper-tree branches, he saw the car slow at the crooked gate in the gaptoothed white-lath fence where red geraniums flared. The car was a pale lavender Montego. The driver, peering anxiously at Ophelia Green's shack out of round dollbaby eyes, was Louise Orton. She saw Dave. The car bucked. Its tires squealed. It roared off up the hill. He turned back and rapped the door hard. The plumbing quit its noise. Footsteps thumped. Ophelia Green yanked open the inner door. "I don't know why you keep bothering me."

"I wouldn't, if you told the truth," Dave said. "You know Anita Orton. She and Lester kept company back before he went to jail. At school and here in La Caleta too. Didn't Lester tell you? They were going to get married."

She clutched the housecoat at her throat. "No," she said. "He's too young. He had to get his schooling."

"All right," Dave said. "Maybe not. Maybe he was afraid of how you'd react. Anita wasn't that smart. Or maybe she simply had different motives. She told her father. He didn't

81

like it. One way he showed that was to erase her name from his insurance policy. The other way he showed it, I think you know. You tell me."

"I don't know what you're talking about," she said. "I wish you'd leave me alone. I work hard. I don't know why anymore. Once I had Lester to work for, hope for. That's all past now. They'll never let some boy that's been a convict be a lawyer. No black boy." Her laugh was brief and bleak. "What a fool I was. To think he'd ever have a chance. To think bringing him up here to raise him would keep him out of trouble."

"It was a safe bet," Dave said.

"There are no safe bets," she said. "Not if you're black. Go away, now. I'm tired. I want my bath. I want my supper. I want to sit and look at the TV till I fall asleep. Is that so much to ask for? I get up every morning at five o'clock."

"Mrs. Green, you know it wasn't 'some other boy' who taped that marijuana under the fender of your son's motorcycle. Lester never told you that."

"Well, it wasn't Lester," she said.

"That's right, but he knew who it was and so do you. You must be aching to tell somebody—after two long years."

She drew a breath, opened her mouth, shut it again. She shook her head. "I don't know what you're talking about."

Dave sighed. Next door the goat bleated. Up the canyon, small birds squabbled in the old trees. The hills cut off the dropping sun. Down here in the shadows, it was turning chilly. He read his watch. Amanda would be giving up on his call. Maybe his father was conscious, able to talk to him. Would he ever know? He looked at the worn black face on the other side of the screen door. "Why should you be afraid of him now? He's dead."

"Who says I'm afraid? Afraid of who?"

"The big man with the badge and gun who sent Lester to prison and came here a week ago Saturday looking for him. On a far more serious charge than possession of marijuana. You told him what you've told me—that Lester wasn't here. And before he could find him, he was murdered."

"Murdered! You talking about Police Chief Orton—is that the Orton you mean? His daughter?" Ophelia Green tried for a disbelieving laugh but her eyes showed fear. "Big, rich people like that? What truck would they have with us? What serious charge?"

"He got a letter. The kind clipped out of magazines and pasted on the page. He didn't like it, didn't believe it. It said someone had his daughter and wanted twenty-five thousand dollars for her safe return. He went to Sangre de Cristo to find her. She wasn't there. But her roommate told him about a telephone call she'd had just before she left. From a boy. For some reason he wondered if that boy had sounded like a Negro. For the same reason, he came here, didn't he? The charge was kidnapping."

Maybe it was the dying light but he didn't think so. She'd gone a sick, ashy color. She turned away her head and groaned. Her hand groped out for the screen-door hook and pried it up. Almost inaudibly she said, "You better come in." He went in. The room still held the heat it had baked in all day. She dropped into an overstuffed chair that was covered by a threadbare flower print. It faced a television set whose plastic case had split and curled. At the ends of the bloated chair arms, her hands hung bony. Her head drooped. She moved it from side to side. "I knew it, just knew it. I should have locked this place up and gone to my

83

sister-in-law in L.A. Thelma. Be no hardship for her. She's a surgical nurse. I shouldn't have listened."

"To Mrs. Orton, you mean?"

"She said there wouldn't be any trouble. Now that he was dead. Now that they had that crazy man locked up for killing him. Nobody else alive knew about that letter. Only her and me. But life's not like that. I knew you'd come along. Not who you'd be—just that you had to be."

"How did you know about the letter?" Dave glanced around the neat, discouraged room. A raffia wastebasket unraveled in a corner. Curled magazines stuck out of it. "Did Lester paste it up here?"

"I told you, I haven't seen him!" she cried. "Anyway, he'd never do such a thing."

"Ben Orton had taken two years of his life. He'd destroyed his future. Becoming a lawyer meant a lot to him. Why wouldn't he want revenge?"

"All black people are not savages," she said. "Black people were building this country before people with names like yours ever stepped off the boat."

"Right," Dave said, "but you don't know whether he pasted up that letter or not, do you? You weren't here. You were out working."

"Only way he'd do that was if she made him," Ophelia Green said. "He didn't hate Ben Orton. Or anybody. Hate you can't live with. I taught him that from a baby. Hate you can only die with. But nobody taught her. And she did hate him—for everything he ever gave her, and he gave her everything."

"Except Lester," Dave said.

Ophelia Green made a scornful sound. "She never wanted Lester. He wanted her but she was just using him

84

to make her daddy mad. To see how far she could stretch his love. Money, cars, clothes, vacations—those were easy for him. He'd always give her what *he* wanted. She had to make him give her something he *didn't* want."

"But you don't know her," Dave said.

Ophelia Green gave him a shamed half smile. She lifted and dropped a hand. "I've known that child since she was three-four years old. I worked for them then. I had to take Lester with me. There was nobody to leave him with. He was always a good boy, played with clothespins and things, quiet in the kitchen, kept out of the way. But she wouldn't let him alone. And she wouldn't play nice, either. Always getting him in trouble. Making him cry."

"Eve," Dave said.

"I didn't like to quit. Mrs. Orton was always very pleasant to me. Her husband didn't like the children playing together but she thought it was sweet. I kept putting it off —what I knew in my heart was right. But I finally saw I had to leave there." She looked grim. "Ought to have left the day I started. Lester was lost to her by then. Broke his heart. He cried and begged me to take him back."

"What about school?" Dave asked.

"By then she wouldn't look at him. Nothing so cruel as little children. I thought he'd die. But after while it looked as if he'd forgotten her. Black, you get used to people treating you one way here and another way there. They don't mean anything by it. I taught him that. I thought it was over. His report cards were good. He had some little friends. He didn't brood anymore."

"She brooded," Dave said. "Where was Jerry in all this?"

"With his daddy. Always with his daddy," she said. "I

don't know how he's going to live without his daddy."

Dave looked at his watch again. He went to the raffia basket and took out the magazines. He put on glasses. "He doesn't know about that ransom note even now. Why not?"

"Anita was making a fool of her daddy," Ophelia Green said. "He didn't want the boy to see him made a fool of."

"Still a boy, is he?" Dave said. They'd used a razor blade to clip out the words. The "$25,000" had been a cake-baking prize offer. "SAFE" was a paper-diaper claim. "And that's what Mrs. Orton told you? That Ben Orton thought the letter was only a hoax? A malicious joke?"

"Oh, he was angry. He was after them. No telling what he'd have done. She came to clear them out of here, if this was where they were hiding. Wanted them to go to Mexico and stay there till he got over how angry he was. But she didn't have any money. He never let her have any."

"It wouldn't have helped Lester." Dave put the glasses away. "He had to report to his parole officer."

"Nothing can help Lester," Ophelia Green said darkly. "He'll go back to jail, like you said. Long years. And for what? For her. And she doesn't give a snap of her fingers for him." The stained eyes looked forlornly at Dave. "He's got good sense. Alone, he'd never step out of line. He knows the price. For blacks it's always twice as high. But for her —if she say do it, he does it."

"They were here, weren't they?" Dave said.

"I guess so. Lester had his key. And his bed"—she broke off and looked at the window where pepper-tree shadows stitched dark lace on the white—"I guess they were in his bed. Looked like it. But they were gone, time I got home." Her eyes pleaded up at Dave. "Chief Orton could have been wrong." The hope in her voice was frail. "Somebody else could have sent that letter."

Dave laid the magazine in her lap. She touched the clipped places, studied them in the poor light. "Yes," she said, "all right." And there were tears on her face when she turned it up to him this time. "But it wasn't meant. It was just a—a game was all it was. Children. A game."

"That everybody lost," Dave said.

At the geranium gate, he heard the whirring noise again. From across the road? The land fell off there, and among ragged weeds crumbling foundation brick showed red where another house had once stood. Crossing, he glanced up the road. No sign of the lavender Montego. But at the nearest bend a Ford van was parked. He'd seen it somewhere this morning. Then, when he'd left Richard Nowell's half an hour ago, hadn't it been among the other cars parked at the top of the road? Frowning to himself, he crunched rubble underfoot between the foundation bricks. But the whirring had stopped. There was a shed that had been left standing when the house had come down. He edged among the bristly stalks of heavy-headed sunflowers. The padlock on the shed door had rusted and fallen loose but something held the door. He peered through weathered siding. There were lumpy shapes within but nothing that moved. He walked around to the back of the shed and squinted in again. He didn't learn anything. He turned. Below, a barranca was thick with creepers—wild cucumber, honeysuckle, morning glory. In the deepening shadows, white flowers showed ghost faces. And there was the glint of bright metal. He looked up. The sky still held a lot of daylight. He started down, careful of his footing. The bank was steep and he kept having to stop and rip loops of vine from around his ankles. He lost sight of the bright metal.

He leaned left, leaned right, narrowing his eyes. Was it glass he saw now? He dropped quickly, stumbling, nearly falling, to the bottom of the barranca, where vines were heaped chin-high. He plunged fingers into the top of the mound and yanked. A thick and heavy mat came away.

Beneath was a small car. Bright green. Brand new.

10

The shiny knob of the motel-room door turned around broken. He pushed the door. A reek of whiskey came at him. He clicked the light switch. Nothing happened. He groped for cords and drew back the curtains on the glass wall. The sky was luminous blue green. So was the water. Their light was enough. Blankets and sheets had been torn off the bed and strewn around. The mattress had been dragged half off the box spring. Drawers had been yanked out and dumped. His suitcase lay like a gutted fish.

He stepped over crumpled suit, shirts, underwear, to lay on the chest the photo of Ben Orton in its envelope, the loaf of carrot bread in its sack, and the distributor head from the little green car. The long mirror over the chest was splintered. The television set lay on its back and stared at the shattered star-spangled white glass of the ceiling light fixture. His bottle of Old Crow had been smashed on the edge of the desk. The whiskey had soaked dark into the carpet.

Next to the toppled nightstand by the bed, among shards of pottery lamp base, lay the telephone. He picked it up, cradled the receiver, lifted it and listened. No dial tone. He pulled at the cord. It came to him limp, ripped loose from the wall. He set the phone on the slope of mattress, found a small pocket-clip screwdriver in the jacket of the fallen suit, and knelt to uncap the little white plastic housing at the foot of the wall and reconnect the wires. He righted the armchair, sat in it, put the phone on his knees, and dialed the hospital.

The floor nurse said, "Mrs. Brandstetter has gone to dinner. She asked me to tell you that your father regained consciousness this afternoon and spoke of you."

"Good," Dave said. "Can I talk to him?"

"Perhaps tomorrow," the nurse said. "His condition is stable now. Doctor is encouraged."

"Tell her I called," Dave said. "Did she go alone?"

"Mr. Sawyer came. With a young man. Hawaiian?"

"Tahitian," Dave said wearily. "Thank you, nurse."

He broke the connection and sat frowning with his finger on the button. Christian Jacques was tall and brown and smooth. With grace, wit, and a stunning smile, he ran a bar and restaurant across the street from Doug's gallery. The Bamboo Raft. It was fronted with fake palm thatch. Fake torches burned beside the door. If you weren't careful, your drink would be laced with coconut milk or papaya juice. Jacques's speech was laced with French. Which was what had got to Doug. Doug had lived and worked in France from the end of the war until de Gaulle expelled NATO. For twenty years, French had been his language—on the job, in shops, taxis, theaters, cinemas, bistros. And in bed.

He'd lived with a young French auto racer. Not hearing the language had to have left in him the kind of space that aches. In Jacques too, no doubt. He'd been born into the language in Papeete and grown up with it in Marseilles and Paris. He and Doug were together so much in order to talk French. And France. Sure they were. Ah, the hell with it.

He dialed 0 and was given the police. But Jerry Orton wasn't there. He wasn't out in his spavined patrol car either. He was off duty till midnight. Dave set the receiver back, took a deep breath, blew it out, and rubbed his eyelids with thumb and knuckle. He was tired and getting his signals mixed. By phone was not how he wanted to talk to young Jerry. The boy. He wanted to walk in on a television baseball game, a tall can of beer, a bag of potato chips. Or the sleep of innocence. He set the phone on the floor, went into the bathroom where the lights still worked, and splashed his face and the back of his neck with cold water. The beer had left a brown taste. He brushed his teeth and rinsed his mouth. He went back through the tumbled room, pulled shut behind him the unlatchable door, walked along the deck above the white boats rocking asleep at their moorings, and went down the steps.

Along the wooden waterfront, candle flames fluttered in colored glass chimneys on the outdoor tables at El Pescador. Above the quiet lap of water beneath his feet, sounds of soft laughter reached him, the clink of silver and glassware. A small red neon sign spelled COCKTAILS against a sky beginning to streak with fire colors. There wasn't time but he wanted a drink anyway. The bar had old curved ship beams, coils of tarry rope, brass ship lanterns. No one sat on the stools. They ate in a farther room where a guitar played—sensible people, people with a grip on their lives, people able to mind their own business. The bartender wore puff sleeves and a silver-embroidered red vest but even with a handlebar mustache he didn't look like Mexico. He looked like Sioux Falls. Dave asked for a drink and the local telephone directory. He put on his glasses. SANGRE DE CRISTO—MADRONE—LA CALETA. The book still wasn't thick. But the listing was there—"Orton, Gerald B., 310 Sandbar Rd., LC."

A plank gallery hung over the bar. Windows were up there. He could look at the sunset on the water. He took his double whiskey up a spiral iron staircase and sat on a canvas-cushioned nail-keg stool at a barrel table. Outside the windows, gulls stood one-legged on a shake roof. He tasted the drink, lit a cigarette, and looked at the ocean and then into the face of the frail old man he'd seen hours ago, drunk in the patio under the jacaranda tree. Tyree Smith. He sat down. He still wore the age-yellowed white linen suit. He was still drunk. Or drunk again. He was clutching a finger-smeared glass with nothing in it.

"I don't want you to misunderstand me," he said.

The bartender called from below, "Smith, I thought I told you to get lost. You been sleeping up there? Get down here. Leave the gentleman alone."

"The gentleman and I are having a drink." Smith's false teeth gave watery clicks. "We're clearing up a misunderstanding. The gentleman is my guest. You have no right to treat me like a bum. I've paid off my bill. Bring us both another drink. Each. Drinks."

"We don't have a misunderstanding," Dave said.

"You were at Mona's gallery. You think I'm some dirty old drunk that goes around molesting women."

"I think you're a good painter," Dave said.

Smith closed an eye. It wasn't a wink. It was an attempt to focus. "Thank you. But you mean 'was.' " He thought about that and shook his head. " 'Were,' " he said. " 'Were' a good painter."

"Those aren't old pictures," Dave said.

"Just finished," Smith said. "But the last. No use—you understand me? Best I could do—best I ever did. But too late. Time ran out. Ground shifted on me."

The bartender's heels gonged on the metal stairs. His head and shoulders appeared. He threw Smith a look of disgust and raised his eyebrows at Dave. Dave shook his head and the bartender brought into sight a pair of drinks on a black-lacquer tray painted with floppy cerise flowers. He set the drinks down and Smith struggled in a pocket. When he drew out his fist, coins rattled to the floor, crumpled bills fell. But he held on to one, smoothed it on the table, eyed the man in the red vest with the insolence of wealth. The man in the red vest grunted, made change, picked up Smith's empty glass, and went off down the clanging stairs.

Smith studied his new drink morosely. "You don't know what it is to live so long. Seventy-one years. You keep finishing with things and you say, 'That's it.' But it never is. There's always something else. You keep having to start over. Well, I have news. Finally you just get too tired. No more. No bleeding more."

"Maybe one?" Dave said. "The crab shell on the rocks. Could you do it again? I'd like to own that."

But Smith didn't hear him. He was listening to his past. He said, "Got out of art school 1925. Began illustrating— books, magazines. Money wouldn't sound like anything today but it bought more then. Hell, I even got married." With a wry, remembering smile, he picked up the fresh glass. The smile faded and he drank. "Depression put an end to that. I painted WPA murals. All scraped off by now.

Married somebody else. She had a lot of wild ideas and just money enough to get us to Hollywood. She was going to be a movie star." He showed the loose teeth in a dingy, sad laugh. "She never even got a screen test. All she got was some kind of kidney infection that killed her. And me? I became head of a studio art department. Kids today are writing books about Hollywood in the thirties. Crazy, they call it. They don't know the half." He drank, set down the glass, squinted one-eyed at Dave again. "You watch much television? I sure as hell do. Don't always turn up the sound. It's the pictures I want. I have to *see*—understand?"

Dave said he thought he did.

"I doubt it," Smith said, "but you watch television some-time. Old movies. You'll catch my name on the credits." He lettered the air with a fragile, dirty white hand. " 'Art Direction, Tyree Smith.' " The hand fell with the slow uncertainty of a scrap of wind-blown paper. "Then came the war. I painted camouflage. Nets to cover whole facto-ries. England mostly. Arms factories. To make them look like enchanted woodlands." He drank again, larynx moving like a knife point in his withered throat. "Enchanted woodlands filled with death." He spoke the tired irony as if he'd lost faith in it. "When it was over, I went back to the studio, but it felt wrong. No fun in it anymore. Or maybe just no fun in me."

"It happened to a lot of us," Dave said.

"You were younger," Smith said. "I was already forty. I told myself, 'I have to do what I want to do. It's now or never. I'm going to paint.' "

"Good for you," Dave said.

"Bad for me," Smith said. "You don't choose painting. Painting chooses you." The new drink was hitting him hard. *Choose* came out *shoes.* And he was teetery on the nail-keg stool. "I didn't know that simple and profound fact. And my ignorance cost me everything—wife, kids, savings, house, car, health, everything." He gripped the edge of the tabletop and leaned at Dave. "And for what? One-man shows in backstreet galleries in towns like Santa Maria, Laguna, Flagstaff. At first. Then a few paintings hanging up to fade in tourist shops. Marked down, marked down again. Lessons to bored housewives without talent." He lifted his glass again and smiled at it wanly. "And booze. No, it didn't help me figure out what was wrong. It helped make figuring out what was wrong unnecessary."

He drank, this time thirstily, and when he set the glass down all that was left in it were ice cubes. He peered at Dave in the deepening shadows under the low rafters.

"But it cost too much. I'd had apartments, then rooms, then rooms in the houses of friends who didn't stay friends long. Then I was sleeping on the beach. And then I was too sick to get up. Hospitals after that. Out sometimes but too sick to work and there was only one cure for the frustration. Booze. Then hospitals again. Veterans' hospitals. Free. Nothing free in this world worth a damn having, my friend. Remember that."

Smith belched. His eyes fell shut. Past him, the sinking sun cast the shadows of the gulls on the window glass. Dave finished his own drink. When he looked up from it, Smith was watching him. Smith looked at the drink Dave hadn't tasted. Dave pushed it across to him.

"Thank you," Smith said. "There was a period when I took fright. I quit drinking. I did my work. Taught at an art institute in Pasadena. There was an article in a national magazine that praises every rotten artist they write about anyway. It sold enough prints of my stuff to buy me a house trailer to keep out the wintry winds. Place to sleep dry.

Wheels to wander on. I quit the institute and wandered, painting boring pictures of boring subjects in a boring style. And knew it and couldn't help it and bought a case of vodka and nearly killed myself."

He drank half of Dave's drink.

"Not ropes and knives and bullets. Unintentionally. Starvation, dehydration, old age." The teeth rattled like dead men's bones. "On the beach at Monterey. When Mona found me. Knew who I was, had been. Took me in, fed me, got me on my feet again. Gave me a little room at the back of her gallery, let me work for my keep. Hell, it wasn't much. Sweep every day, put up a nail now and then, screw in a light bulb, water the plants out front, frame some tourist's lousy seascape once in a while.

"She said if I'd paint when I was strong again, she'd give me a show. Place did a middling business. Pretty setting—not heaven, but more than I deserved. I knew that. I pulled myself together and tried to work again. Shook too much. Had to drink to get the shakes down to where I could draw a line, hold a brush. But there was some point to working now—to pay Mona back. She kept the bottle, doled out the drinks, and slowly the pictures got done. Best I ever did. Can't account for it." Smith shook his head in wonderment. "I started seeing things like I'd never seen them before. I got them down on paper that way. All I needed was time." He scowled. "Then that big bullneck cop blundered in and wrecked it. Love!" He choked on the word. "The woman is almost forty. Love is a swindle. Grown man is supposed to know that. Not him. Gray-haired, overweight, father of grown children, for God's sake. But from that first minute, it was candlelight and gypsy violins all the way. Sickening."

"Ben Orton," Dave said.

"I raise my glass"—Smith had trouble locating it and

getting his fingers around it but he managed at last to hoist it at a dangerous tilt, ice cubes rattling—"to the little woman that killed that loudmouth yahoo. With only one reservation." He drank from the glass, set it down with a bang that didn't mean anything except bad aim, brushed at his mouth with a limp hand. "She waited too long."

"Who?" Dave asked.

But Smith's attention had slipped. He had lowered his chin to tabletop level and was sliding his hands toward the glass like a kid trying to catch a sitting toad. He sighted on the glass one-eyed. He smiled. The hands closed—but next to the glass, not on it. He made a noise, sat straight, and with no trouble at all picked up the glass and drank from it. And fell off the stool. It was a noisy fall. The stool went over too and the glass broke.

"What the hell?" the bartender said.

"It's all right," Dave said. He knelt beside the rickety old man. He had hit his head. The teeth had jumped out and lay glistening pink on the planks. He didn't seem any more alive than they were. Dave felt for the beat of life in the crooked blue vein of his scraggy neck. It was there. He lifted the old head. It felt eggshell-fragile in his hand. Smith opened his eyes.

"His wife," he said, "plump little blond."

"Never mind that now," Dave said. "Are you all right?"

"Drunk as hell." Smith grinned, looked panicked, covered his mouth. "Teeth. Where my teeth?" He pushed at Dave feebly, rolling his eyes at the planks. He snatched up the teeth, rubbed them on his jacket, made a horrible, gaping face and set them back in place. He struggled to get up. Dave helped him. Smith stared down at the shattered glass, the clean curved edges glittering in the ruddy light. "Shame," he said. "Awful waste."

97

"You've had enough. Let's get you out of here." Dave began to help Smith down the stairs. He was light to manage, bones like sticks, no flesh on them to speak of. And he didn't quarrel with being helped. He let it happen. The twisted stairs were narrow and both of them jarred the rails and got their legs tangled but Smith went on talking.

"She had a little revolver. Hoo, was she mad!"

"What revolver?" The bartender put a foot on the steps and reached up to help. "Who's got a revolver?"

"No one here," Dave said. "It's all right. I have him." They reached floor level. Smith pulled free of him, poking into pockets again, muttering. "Tip the man."

"All I want from you," the bartender said, "is for you to get lost." He waved a puff-sleeved arm at windows that showed the sunset people at the candlelit tables. "Go fall off the deck over there."

"Where does he live?" Dave asked. "Do you know?"

The bartender squinted. "What are you—a Boy Scout?"

"It's a small town," Dave said. "Wherever it is can't be far out of my way."

The bartender went back to his bottles. "Take the road that cuts off at the school. You'll hit a big stand of eucalyptus. Other side of that, he's got a trailer. Goddam eyesore. Ought to be a law."

Mumbling, Smith fell toward the bar, waving a twenty-dollar bill. Dave caught him in mid-fall, swung him around, steered him toward the door, taking the bill out of his hand and tucking it back into his pocket. Outside, diners looked up briefly, looked down again embarrassed. Except for two. They stared. One was Mona Windrow in a white knitted shawl, the other was Al Franklin in a new denim leisure suit, beard trimmed, long hair clubbed back, nails showing no trace of motor grease. Mona Windrow pushed back her chair and started to rise, distress in her eyes, pity. He reached across and stopped her. Then they both recognized Dave. He nodded to them. Mona Windrow didn't return the nod. She was looking reproach at Franklin. But Franklin nodded. As Dave guided the unseeing Smith past them, Franklin even spoke. "Evening." It didn't mean much but it didn't quite mean nothing.

In the rental car, slumped askew in the bucket seat, safety strap bunching up the linen jacket, head bumping the window glass, hands fallen to his lap palms-up in a gesture of emptiness, eyes shut, Smith still couldn't stop talking. "She'd really worked herself up, shaky hands, squeaky voice. Told him she'd kill him if he didn't leave Mona alone." Smith made a sour sound, opened blurry eyes, turned his head to wince at the flicker of hard red light through the ragged tree trunks. "Wasted her chance with words. She should have pulled that trigger. He knew her better than she knew herself, walked up to her, took away the gun, told her he'd do as he damn pleased and if she didn't like it, she could leave him." Smith snorted. "He knew she never would."

The bartender had been right. The trailer was an eyesore. Dented aluminum, spattered with dried mud, a square of rain-stained cardboard where a window had been, it hung on a weedy point of land above jagged black rocks the tide was backing away from. Three respectable-looking campers kept their distance, sheltering at the edge of the trees. There was a lone telephone booth. From wooden poles with tin meter boxes limp wires fed electricity to the campers and trailer. Smith had passed out. Dave opened the old man's door, undid the safety strap, and hauled him to his feet.

The inside of the trailer was a shambles of crumpled drawings, pizza tins, wrappers. Dave lowered Smith onto a bunk heaped with dirty clothes and dirtier blankets. Museum prints of Cézanne apples and Hokusai insects were pinned up over it, faded, flyspecked. Smith began to snore. Turning away, Dave bumped a portable television set. About to shut the trailer door after him, he saw Smith struggle up to switch the machine on. Color splashed the soiled white suit before he collapsed on the bunk again. No sound came from the set. The sound came from Smith.

"Long as his wife knew anyway, Orton wanted his mistress someplace he didn't have to drive half the night to get to. He paid for the move, lease on the patio place. Nothing too good for Mona. And that so-called brother of hers." Smith chuckled. Lecherously. "Brother! I emptied the wastebaskets. I saw letters he wrote to her. Those weren't from any brother. Hottest stuff you ever read. Worth keeping."

"Franklin?" Dave asked.

He didn't get an answer. He heard a clinking sound he didn't understand. Then Smith began to snore again. Loud and steady. Dave stepped in and shook him. He didn't wake. From a glass of green water on the floor the teeth grinned. Dave went out and shut the door.

11

Sandbar Road took him into marshes. The planks of a wooden bridge rumbled under the hard little car wheels. The bridge crossed an inlet edged and islanded with reeds. The water lay calm and glossed with red from the last light of the sun. Far out on it a rowboat looked lonely. A sign at the end of the bridge read LA CALETA STATE PARK—U.S. WILDFOWL REFUGE. The blacktop veered and went among old live oaks hung with moss. Houses clustered there, half a dozen of them, stucco, low-roofed, bristly with TV antennas, economy cars in the driveways. He parked at the mailbox numbered 310.

Sand was soft and fine under his shoes as he crossed a yard where some kind of creeping succulent tried to flower before it was buried. Two cars were in this driveway and another in the garage. He pushed the doorbell. On the door someone had mounted a carving of a bird. It was clumsy work but he guessed it was meant to be a sea eagle. That might have been a fish in its claws. The light was poor. He waited on a woven reed mat dyed with flowers, but no one came to let him in.

He wandered around the side of the house. At the back, lengths of muslin hung on lines stretched between iron clothespoles. The material had a stiff look about it and the patterns were unfinished. He touched a hanging corner. Somebody was trying batik. The sand of the yard sloped down to a sturdy wooden jetty that thrust from clumps of rushes. He walked out on it. The boards were stained with oil. The lines that lay on them were strong and used. There was a red gasoline can stenciled LA CALETA POLICE. Off across the inlet, a flock of ducks made a wide, quick-winged circle and came down splashing. The noise of their voices was harsh in the stillness. A human voice came thinly through, a female voice. "Hello!" Someone waved from the rowboat and it came toward him, the oars shedding drops of red and silver. For what he didn't know, but he waited.

The pair of cameras on straps around her neck looked wrong because she wore an antique white dress with plackets and gussets, fringes and lace. It was long and the hem was wet from the bilge that sloshed in the flat bottom of the boat. She was barefoot. Dave crouched and took the painter from her and wound it around a cleat. He helped her up onto the jetty. She didn't appear to be wearing anything under the dress. She had a lot of pale yellow hair, part of it carelessly pinned up, part hanging loose. She'd put on no makeup. He recognized, but only just, the woman who had touched Jerry Orton's hand in the funeral film. That one had been neatly groomed and could be mistaken for a college girl. This one had to be years older than her husband.

"Did you want me?" she said. "I'm Frances Orton."

"I wanted Jerry Orton," Dave said. "Where is he?"

102

"Gone off." She waved a hand toward the ocean. "Fishing with cormorants. In the launch. They put collars on the birds, you know, so they can't swallow. They burn torches to attract the fish. Romantic."

"And illegal," Dave said.

She shrugged. "Boys will be boys." She went off up the sand, tall for a woman and a little ghostly in the dying light and the 1905 dress. Trudging made her hips look heavy. "What did you want? Perhaps I can help." She paused and fingered the hanging muslin. "Do you know anything about batik? It's done with wax and dyes, a sort of stenciling. Only it's not turning out the way it looks in the book."

"Wait till it's finished," Dave said. "Is there a radio on this launch? It's important."

"On the launch," she said, "but not here. It's the police launch." She pushed open a blue door with seagulls painted on it. "What's it about?"

"His father's death," Dave said. "I'm from the insurance company." He gave her a card. "When will he be back?"

"Oh, not for hours. He doesn't go on duty again till midnight." In the dark doorway, she tilted her head. "May I take a message? I look crazy but I'm not. I was a college instructor. That's how I met Jerry. A crash course in Spanish for police and sheriff's officers. I fight it but deep down I'm responsible."

"It's complicated," Dave said.

She laughed and walked into the house. "Then explain it to me." A pale shadow, she took off the cameras by their straps and set them somewhere out of his line of sight. "Come in." She pushed at her hair. "If you think it's too much for my wandering wits, I'll write it down."

"How well do you know his sister?" He stepped into a room that was the width of the house. The rug was big and

103

shapeless and hand hooked—seagulls again, with clouds and waves this time. A loom, a potter's wheel, a drawing table took up most of the space, along with a butcher-block bench heaped with lenses and tripods and light meters, yellow boxes of film and printing paper, hanks of bright yarn and earth-color twine, and brushes and paint pots. But in a corner, a Sears Roebuck couch and easy chair in tough blue plaid faced a TV set that held up a terra-cotta sculpture of a leaping porpoise, not very well done. Macrame work hung ragged on the walls. So did a blurred enlargement of a photo of what might have been a gray whale or an overturned and barnacled ship's hull. "How much of a radical is she?"

"Oh, that's only an act to upset her father." Frances Orton went around a counter crowded with dying houseplants into a shadowy kitchen where beach birds were painted on cupboard doors. "I never knew a girl so desperate for a man's love." She bent out of sight and made kitcheny rattles. "Of course, he gave it all to Jerry."

"And how did Jerry take it?" Dave asked.

"For granted." Her voice echoed hollow from some low cabinet. "As the lucky ones of this world take everything." She rose again beyond the plants and frowned at him. "Or do you mean his father's death? That's what you're here about. He took that badly. Gods are not supposed to die."

"He's out enjoying himself tonight," Dave said.

"With friends very like his father." She came from the kitchen with a half-gallon glass jug of wine and a pair of lopsided clay mugs. "Men made by his father in his father's image. Ugh." She handed Dave one of the mugs. "From my potting period. You can see why I gave it up." She splashed wine into the mugs and set the jug on the cluttered bench.

104

Dave said, "There were other periods, weren't there? Rug making, wood carving, sculpture?"

"Stop. You couldn't begin to name them all."

"What did your father-in-law think of them?"

"And my funny clothes?" She walked away, dragging the wet, sandy hem of the old dress toward the couch. "He ordered me to shape up, and when I ignored him he tried to wreck my marriage." She dropped onto the couch and tucked up her feet. "You see, when Jerry and I met, I was still reacting against my upbringing. I was the most conventional girl in the world." She looked at Dave over her shoulder. "Come sit down."

He took the easy chair and set the cup on the margin of vinyl tile the seagull rug didn't cover. He didn't want the wine. "What kind of upbringing?"

"Crazy poets and crazier musicians, colored candles stuck in Chianti bottles, suppers out of cardboard boxes from the corner taco stand, drunks and fights, rehearsals till dawn, strangers sleeping in the bathtub, unmade beds and unpaid bills, escapes down midnight freeways in hundred-dollar cars." She smiled a crooked smile. "Any questions?"

"So you taught school," Dave said, "and married a cop."

"But when I'd spent a couple of years with Louise Orton and a dozen other police wives and their children"—she lifted her cup at him wryly—"you see your husband never"—she drank and her look traveled the room—"I began to miss the way I'd grown up. I started painting, making lampshades, dressing up in garage-sale rags. Ben Orton ordered Jerry to divorce me. His wife and her friends cut me dead. I don't miss them. Especially not that fat backwoods Hitler, Ben. All I need is Jerry. I counted on his not minding, and he didn't, he doesn't. I have advice for women seeking husbands—with a law-enforcement officer, what you see is what you get."

"Including indifference to laws that don't suit him," Dave said. "Minor ones, like fishing with cormorants or slashing the tires of an unwanted stranger in town. Or major ones, like burning down the local radical newspaper."

She cleared her throat and gave a recitation. "The courts don't understand the problem. The legislators don't understand the problem. The police officer has to deal with the problem, face to face, day in, day out. It's often a matter of his life, a split-second decision. The judgment as to what he has to do can't wait for laws to be written and passed and a string of courts to make up their minds. He has to protect himself and the public who depend on him. Whether they like it or not." Her mouth twitched. "End of creed."

Dave grinned. "I can tell your belief runs deep."

"His does," she said grimly, "as his father's did before him." She sighed, shook her head. "Mine doesn't matter. What did you want me to tell Jerry? What's Anita done now?"

"Why wasn't she at the funeral?" Dave asked.

"What? Why—she had the flu. That's what Louise said. She was sick in bed. At college. Sangre de Cristo." Frances Orton blinked. "Wasn't she? Anyway—what does it have to do with her father's death?"

"She was in bed but not sick and not at college. With a boy named Lester Green in his mother's house up the canyon across the highway."

She frowned. "What are you talking about?"

"I warned you it was complicated," Dave said. "You don't know who Lester Green is?"

"No. Wait." She looked thoughtful and gulped wine. "A black boy—right? Motorcycle? Arrested for dope?"

"On one of those split-second decisions you mentioned," Dave said. "When Anita's father learned she and Lester had taken out a marriage license."

She put her feet on the floor. "You're joking."

"You don't really think so," Dave said. "You're a young female relative. She must have told you how badly her father was treating her? Not only framing and locking up her boyfriend but disowning her—taking her name off his insurance policy. I don't know what else."

"Nothing else," Frances Orton said. "Not even that much. What I heard, I heard from Jerry. And it wasn't anything about any boyfriend." She emptied her wine cup and went to the jug. "Just that Ben was furious with Anita again and wasn't buying her the car he'd promised." She tilted wine into her cup again, looked at him eyebrows-up, and, when he shook his head, recapped the jug. "She kept away from me." Frances Orton laughed briefly and without amusement. "Thought I'd betrayed my class. If only she'd known how my father twisted himself into knots inside with envy for the poets who made it, while he failed in back rooms of funky bookshops with beer cans and sleeping bags on the floor and everyone too stoned to listen while he read. What he really wanted was to write a sleazy best-seller and have sex all day long by a swimming pool in Bel Air with starlets. He was always being praised for his integrity. He'd have sold it in a minute, only no one wanted to buy." She'd been staring out the window at the inlet. She turned to him. "Sorry. No. I didn't know. Jerry didn't know either, I suspect. His father was always keeping things from him." She dropped onto the couch again, tucked up her feet again.

107

"I thought that was strange in a man with no sensitivity whatever."

"Keeping things such as?" Dave asked.

"His women," she said.

"He wasn't protecting Jerry," Dave said, "he was protecting his image, the myth of Ben Orton, champion of law and order, the family, the flag—the things, as his wife told me this morning, that make America great. Which did not include adult movies, homosexual police officers, and most specially not an underground paper."

"You keep coming back to that," she said. "It burned, that's all I know."

"And all Jerry knew too, I'll bet. Let me tell you why." He told her about his day and what he'd learned. It took time. He wound up with, "And, sure enough, this afternoon Louise Orton drove up to Ophelia Green's to warn her I was in town and asking about Anita. Mrs. Green didn't know I knew that. She kept on lying. But those kids have been at her place right along. They're there now. Anita's ears must have been burning behind the door when she heard what Mrs. Green said about her." He frowned at Frances Orton. "Her father did give her that car. A Gremlin."

"Lately. For staying in school and not making waves."

"I don't think so. Have Jerry ask her when he sees her tonight. It was a bribe to keep her away from Lester Green when he got out of prison. She must have promised. Only why would he believe her?"

"She's a female," Frances Orton said, "and he loved her. What's so important about the car?"

"It's hidden in a ravine," Dave said, "across from the house. Under vines."

She shook her head. "No. It doesn't make sense. Why

108

hide the car? Why hide themselves? A man's in jail for the murder. The case against him is open and shut. They surely can't enjoy being huddled up in some stuffy little house. For a stupid, adolescent prank that misfired? For how long, for heaven's sake? Forever?"

"It misfired," Dave said, "but not the way you mean."

"Oh, no." Her eyes widened. "Oh, surely not."

"That's why I'm here." Dave pushed to his feet. The sunset light off the water struck his eyes. They hurt. He hurt all over. He tried to count to himself how many hours it had been since he'd slept. His mind wouldn't do the sum. "Please tell him as soon as he gets back." Dave stepped out onto the sand.

She called after him. "Where can he find you?"

"He knows," Dave said.

She came to the door. "What if they've run away? What if you scared them off?"

"That car won't go," Dave said.

12

Not even an edge of light showed the horizon when he got back. He left the rental car up a side street. Limping toward the glow above the shake roofs of the waterfront, he passed the Ford van that had bothered him on the hilltop behind Nowell's and again down the dusty road near Ophelia Green's. He craned to peer through the window. Nothing lay on the seats. In the rear, the cargo was darkness. He turned away. It didn't matter now. It was over. It was certainly over for Lester Green. He wished that made him feel good but it didn't. Frances Orton was right—something about it didn't add up. He shrugged. Let Jerry Orton work it out. It wasn't Dave Brandstetter's business anymore.

The candle flames still flickered in the colored glass chimneys on the tables outside El Pescador. The breeze was soft, steady, cool. Beyond the white railings of the deck, the masts of the moored boats tilted shiny against the blackness of the bay. Pointing at what? He squinted and made out a few stars. They weren't his business either. He wished all the tables were empty. Instead, at the farthest one, where they'd splashed the white cloth with red wine, college boys looked pale and laughed loud but not long and not together. Celebrating what—their first adult mistake? And at the nearest table, where he'd left them, Mona Windrow and Al Franklin nursed brandy snifters.

They had cups of coffee too, and Franklin smoked a slim cigar. He leaned back in his chair, paying her grave attention. She read aloud from a typed list open on the cloth where her plate had been. Dave heard her say "museum" and "curator" and "Arkansas." There was no way to the door but past them. He hoped they were too busy to notice. Franklin raised his odd blue eyes and jerked a nod but swung his attention back to the woman right away. Plainly he wanted an encounter as much as Dave did. Then she looked up. And drew a sharp breath. And pushed back her chair. A patchwork knitting bag slid off her lap and spilled on the deck. Envelopes. Institutional checks.

"Oh, wait, please." She came after him.

"He's all right," Dave said. "Safe in his trailer."

"I owe you an explanation," she said, "after this noon. You see, when I found him, he was sick, helpless—"

Franklin said, "Time comes when the only smart thing is to cut your losses. Mona—the nice man knows that."

"Is he—?" she began. "Did he—?"

Franklin said, "She means, he talks too much."

"He's had quite a life," Dave said.

"I'm afraid he's angry at me," she said, "but—"

"He's grateful to you," Dave said.

She studied his face, mistrustful, looking for irony.

"What did I tell you?" Franklin said. "Drink, Mr.—?"

"Brandstetter. No, thanks. I'd better eat while the kitchen's still open." He went inside.

The kitchen was closed. By folding a twenty-dollar bill into the palm of a tailored and unsmiling maitre d' he got the kitchen opened again. He also got a smile, a table, and a roomful of silence. In a corner, a spotlight shone on a microphone, a tall black stool, and a closed guitar case. A waiter in a red jacket began bending at the empty tables, blowing out the candles. With a glance at Dave, the maitre d' made him stop. Dave ate lettuce with oil and tarragon vinegar, a slab of grilled swordfish with lemon butter. He drank half the icy Chablis from a slender green bottle and, when he left, carried the bottle along.

This meant to him that he was drunk. That he was drunk meant to him that he was very tired. His knees told him the same thing when he climbed the steps to the motel deck. Then he pushed the door with the broken lock and felt awake and sober—because he saw himself reflected in the glass of the television set, and he had left the television set lying on its back. Not much light reached here from the clear glass globes on posts along the waterfront below, but it let him see that the chest drawers were back in place. He hadn't told the motel office. If they'd found out for themselves, they'd have fixed the lock. And the lights. He slid a hand inside and moved the switch. Nothing happened.

He didn't feel brave. He felt annoyed. He changed his grip on the bottle and took a step through the doorway. The bed jounced and he saw eye whites, a gleam of teeth, a form coming at him. *Lester Green,* he thought. *I could have slept in the car.* And he swung the bottle. At the head. But the bottle surprised him with its weight. It didn't get that high. Also it was slippery. It glanced off a shoulder and left his hand. Someplace in the dark it struck a wall and the floor.

There was a yelp. A black sprawl twisted and whimpered at his feet. He ran to the bathroom and switched on the light. Hard white enamel covered the door. The light glared off it into the room.

From beside the bed, Cecil Harris looked at him—the skinny black college boy from KSDC-TV. His eyes were round. He clutched his shoulder. "Shee-it, man," he said reproachfully, "what did you do that for?"

"I can't imagine," Dave said. "I don't, usually."

"I thought you'd be glad to see me." Cecil pushed to his feet, grimacing, moving the arm to see if it worked.

"I guess you did," Dave said. "Otherwise you'd have your clothes on."

Cecil looked down at himself and looked up, smiling shyly. "We did the signals, didn't we? This morning. I knew and you knew and you knew I knew—right?"

"It happens," Dave said. "I'm still surprised."

"That's what I meant it to be," Cecil said. "A nice surprise." He glanced at the bed. The red, white, and blue spread held the long, narrow imprint of his body. "Found the door open and it came to me to wait." He passed Dave and crouched. "Had the loaf of bread." He came up from the corner with the bottle. "Now I got the wine." He smiled. "And thou." He rubbed his shoulder.

"How bad is that?" Dave asked him.

"I'll be black and blue for life," Cecil said. "Man, you are no housekeeper. I had a lot of tidying up to do."

"People keep helping themselves to my room."

"The same ones that slashed your tires?" Cecil went into the bathroom and came out with two of the plastic glasses. He set them on the chest, uncapped the bottle, and poured the pale wine. He pulled the loaf of bread out of its sack and tore it in his hands. He passed a chunk to Dave and handed him a glass, looking at him with earnestness and pain. "Man, what I want is not to break bread and drink wine with you."

"It's a way to keep out of trouble," Dave said. "Did you see who slashed my tires?"

"I even took a picture," Cecil said. "A movie."

"Lose it," Dave said. "You know what happens to young blacks who cross the La Caleta police."

"Honkies, too, look like." Cecil lifted the plastic glass. "Here's to that trouble you mentioned." He drank and showed surprise. "Oh, that is good wine." He bit into the bread and spat it out. "Christ, what is that?" He peered at the lump in his palm. He took away Dave's chunk. "Don't eat that. Bound to kill you." He went into the bathroom again. The toilet flushed.

Dave stepped to the doorway. Cecil bent at the basin, noisily washing out his mouth. In the white dazzle of tile, paint, mirror, the detail of how he was made showed. Out of clothes, he didn't look skinny. His face where he shaved was rough. The rest of him was smooth. He groped for a towel, scrubbed his face, caught Dave staring, and grinned. They hadn't tamed his grin for the camera yet. It showed his gums.

"You followed me," Dave said.

"And I'm not even a masochist." Cecil hung up the towel, switched off the light, and reached for Dave. "Let's get into trouble now, okay?"

Dave turned away. "I'm too old for you. I'm drunk. I haven't slept in nearly forty hours. And I have a phone call to make."

"It's late," Cecil said. "They'll be asleep."

Dave carried the phone to the open door where the deck lamps below let him just make out the circle of numbers.

He held the receiver with a shoulder and dialed. In the dark room, the bedspread billowed up like a night sail and fell. The bed creaked. "You know where to find me, old man," Cecil said.

On the phone the doctor said, "We're doing our best."

"They called you in, did they?" Dave said. "This afternoon they told me he was better."

"He could rally again," the doctor said.

"But you don't think he will," Dave said.

"I wish it were morning," the doctor said.

"Don't they die in the morning?"

"They don't seem to. Not as often."

"Once is all it takes," Dave said, and hung up. He leaned in the doorway, hearing the water lap around the boats, seeing the masts sway. The bay was glassy black. Lonely lights were scattered along the curving shore. The hills rose dark behind them. There were more stars now. He carried the phone back to the stand and set it there with a faint jingle of its bell. He sat on the bed and tugged off the canvas shoes. "How's your father?"

"How is anybody in Detroit?" The words came muffled.

Dave pulled the denim tunic off over his head. "You don't miss him?"

"Man, I don't remember anything about him." The bed jounced. Warm hands were on Dave's shoulders. Warm breath was on the back of his neck. A kiss. "Why should I miss anybody? Here. Now."

Dave sighed. "Just a minute." He hiked his butt and shoved the pants down. He kicked them away, turned, and took Cecil's face in his hands. All he could see of it were the eyes. But his mouth found the mouth he couldn't see and kissed it. He said, "You have a long lifetime before you. I hope that during that long lifetime you never have occasion to be as tired as I am right now. To make the following announcement saddens me. I hope it saddens you, though I shouldn't, and it shouldn't. But when my head hits that pillow, there's no way I'm going to do anything but sleep."

Cecil's laugh was soft and wicked. "We'll see."

The bed moved. The warmth went from beside him. He moaned and opened his eyes. Colors shifted in the night room. There was an electronic twittering. He pushed up on an elbow and winced at the ache in his muscles. Cecil crouched in front of the television set. On the screen, cartoon dinosaurs melted into a pool of crude oil. Bright rubber automobiles passed. A dinosaur peered from a gas tank.

"They figure out cute ways"—Cecil came back to the bed —"to tell us we're all doomed." He fell beside Dave, pulled Dave down, hung an arm across him.

"I've read about the need," Dave said, "of today's young for constant visual stimulation but this is—"

Cecil's hand stopped his mouth. "Wait," he said. "Coming up is the second part of my surprise."

Dave took the hand, kissed it, put it lower where he wanted it. He turned onto his side, shut his eyes and fitted himself into Cecil's angles. "I liked the first part," he mumbled, and fell asleep again.

But not for long. Cecil was shaking his shoulder. "Wake up. Here it comes now. Your TV debut. You don't know how beautiful you are."

Daisy Flynn spoke his name. He sat up and squinted at the phosphorescent picture. A lean, blond man in blue denim walked beside Hector Rodriguez through the dappled leaf shadow of the nursery. Daisy Flynn's voice was saying ". . . business partner of Cliff Kerlee, now awaiting trial for the slaying of La Caleta Police Chief Benjamin J.

116

Orton." Now Hector Rodriguez flinched alone in sunlight and kept rubbing his smooth brown chest. He said, "I told him the same thing I told the officers. Cliff didn't do it. He was here with me when it happened." The camera had shaken Rodriguez's nerve. The lean, blond man in denim sat drinking beer on Richard T. Nowell's terrace. The picture had fuzzy edges and it jittered. Dave looked at Cecil, who shrugged.

"That hillside is loose. My feet kept slipping. I balanced it on a rock. But that's a telephoto shot. I really held it steadier than that."

"The whirring noise," Dave said.

"I thought you had me in that shed across from Mrs. Green's house," Cecil said. "I nearly pissed."

"The Ford van." Dave stared without seeing at Dick Nowell's tight little smile and didn't hear the man's words. He set his feet on the rug. "You little sneak."

"Come on!" Cecil said. "You told me it was my beat."

"No—you told me. I should have listened." He stood up. Too fast. It made his head hurt. "There are some pills in my shaving kit," he said. "Get them for me, please." Grimacing, he bent to switch off the set, then changed his mind. He straightened up carefully and Cecil put a damp glass into his hand.

"How many?" he said, and, when Dave held up fingers, shook two into his palm. "How come antihistamine?"

"It's a wine headache." Dave put the pills into his mouth and washed them down with water from the glass. "Wine is rich in histamines. That's why you get wine headaches. Easiest headaches in the world to cure." He gave back the glass. "You, on the other hand—"

"It's all true," Cecil said.

117

"It would be just as true if you hadn't taken pictures of it," Dave said.

He stood among the drooping branches of the old pepper tree on the stoop at Ophelia Green's, leaning a hand on the doorframe, talking to an old black screen. Then there was the stoic, high-cheekboned face of Ophelia Green. Then came her words: "Just an insurance man, is all I know. I can't afford any insurance. Nothing about my son. I don't know anything about it." And the door with the cracked pane closed.

Daisy Flynn looked out at the naked pair of them and said something about a Channel Ten Latenews Exclusive. And there was a poorly lit shot of the little green car in its grave of green vines, and words about the car being registered to Benjamin J. Orton. "On tomorrow's morning news, KSDC-TV expects to bring you an interview with David Brandstetter on the purpose of his—" Dave shut the set off.

"You want to take the tape recorder out from under the bed now?" he said. "Bending makes my head hurt."

"Shit." Cecil jerked his own head—so hard it made the whole slender length of him jump. "What kind of creep do you think I am?"

"The kind that only does his job," Dave said.

"Like you," Cecil jeered. "Oh, yes. Don't try to—"

The telephone rang. Cecil looked at it scared. Young and bare-assed in the wrong place at the wrong time. Something else scared Dave. He saw the shadowy hospital room. He saw Carl Brandstetter's big, handsome head over against the bars of the high bed. He saw a nurse untape the wires from the stilled hands, pull away the oxygen tubes from the face. He saw orderlies in rumpled white wheel in a shiny trolley. To make himself stop seeing, he went and picked up the phone.

118

"I didn't know who you were." The words came slurred. "Why didn't you tell me? Why did I have to see it on the news?" False teeth rattled. "Thought we were friends."

"Smith?" For a second, Dave held the receiver away and stared at it. "Is this Tyree Smith?"

"I could have told you who killed the son of a bitch," Smith said. "All you had to do was ask me."

"You told me," Dave said. "Mrs. Orton—remember?"

Something banged the phone at Smith's end. A glass? Bottle, more likely. "You don't want to pay"—Smith belched—"too much attention to my dramatic improv—" He backed off and tried the word again. "Improvisations."

"You mean she didn't threaten him?"

"Way I told you," Smith said. "But, face it—she couldn't step on an ant." The banging happened again. He must have dropped the receiver. It swung on its wire against the glass of the lonely booth under the eucalyptus trees. Then Smith had it again. "My car's missing. You come here."

"That newscast was stale," Dave said. "I'm off the case now. The police are handling it. Phone them."

"You know better than that," Smith said.

"Look," Dave said, "it's late. Can't this wait till—"

There was a clatter and the receiver hummed in Dave's ear. He set the phone down and picked up his pants. "You're wrong. I never slept with anybody to get an interview."

"Neither did I," Cecil cried.

"Don't feel bad." Dave tottered on one leg, getting into the denims. "You'll get niftier with more experience."

"No, man, please." Cecil reached out. "Come on. It wasn't like that." Tears glistened in his eyes. "I would have followed you if there wasn't any story. I would have been waiting here like I was."

119

"But there is a tape recorder." Dave zipped his fly.

"In the van," Cecil said desperately, "in the van."

Dave untangled the denim tunic from the sheets and blankets. "In case I had anything to say." He pulled the tunic on over his head. "In a good mood." He sat on the bed and reached for his shoes. "In the morning."

"No." Cecil dropped to his knees in front of him. "You are wrong, wrong, wrong." He tried to work the clasp of the denims. "Let me show you."

Dave caught his wrists. "You're only making it worse."

Cecil sat back on his heels. Crying like a child. "What can I do? You want me to say I love you? All right—I love you. Sounds like some stupid song. This is real. When I saw you up on the mountain this morning, talked to you—it had to happen, man. I had to get it on with you. Christ, can't you understand?"

Dave said, "You should stop talking."

"I can't talk to you, I can't touch you, what do you want?" Cecil jumped up. "Use your brains." He flung out an arm at the dark television set. "If it was like you say, why would I turn on the news for you to see what I did? You were asleep, man. You'd never have seen it. Maybe I did wrong. Looks like it. But it never crossed my mind you'd take it like this. That's how come I woke you up and showed you." His hands were out, begging. "Didn't I show you?"

Dave stood up wearily. "Come here," he said. Cecil trembled in his arms. He stroked the sleek, long back. He gently kissed the mouth that was salty with tears. "Put on your clothes," he said. "I have to go someplace, and if I try to drive myself, I'll fall asleep."

13

He woke when the ungiving little car began to jolt over potholes in the road through the eucalyptus grove. The crunch of peeled bark and dry seedpods under the tires was loud in the midnight silence. Twigs snapped. He straightened stiffly in the bucket seat, rubbed the back of his neck, worked his tongue around in a dry mouth. The steel and glass of the phone booth glinted in the headlights for a second. And here was the wedge of bare ground. With the dash lights in his eyes, he couldn't make out the campers under the trees, but there in the headlight glare was Tyree Smith's trailer on the point. Its door hung open.

"We're here," Dave said. Cecil pushed the brake pedal. The car came to a halt, tilted in a rut. Cecil switched off the engine, and the thud and splash of surf reached them. Dave unbuckled his seat belt and climbed out. Cecil cut the headlights. "No," Dave said. "Leave those." Cecil switched the

121

headlights on again. Dave walked off. "This shouldn't take long."

He climbed bent aluminum steps and put his head in at the door. The smell was of mildewed clothes and moldy food—no change in that. But he didn't hear snoring. He pawed around for a light switch and there didn't seem to be one. He stepped inside and flicked his cigarette lighter. The flame showed him an empty bunk. "Smith?" he said. To nobody. He went down the steps and squinted across the acre. Nothing moved. The big trees rustled in the cold breath of the sea. He walked around the trailer. The footing was bad. He twisted an ankle. He crouched. Under the trailer the lighter showed him beer cans, blown wrappers, weeds. He put the lighter away, brushed sand off his hands. "Smith?"

Somewhere Cecil said, "Shit. Oh, shit."

Dave got to his feet. The headlights showed the boy's long legs in yellow jeans. He was standing on the point. "What is that?" He sounded scared. "Down there." Dave stumbled to him. Cecil gripped his arm. The long fingers pinched. "Man, what *is* that?"

The black tide gulped and hissed around the rocks. And something floated on it, white and shifting. "That," Dave said, "is a sad old man in a sad old linen suit. He was tired of starting over. Help me down there."

But when he got his rope soles planted on two rocks, Smith was still out of his reach. The headlight beams shot off to sea above his head. They only made it darker down there. The rocks were black to start with. He bent this way, that way, groping out for handholds. His legs were spread too wide. A bottle kept clinking. He couldn't see it.

"I better come down," Cecil said.

"Never mind," Dave said. "The police will have a grappling hook. Help me back up."

They came without sirens but there was no way not to hear them. Rusty manifolds roared, valves clattered, a bent fan blade sang against a radiator. Their headlights flickered among the ragged tree trunks. They jounced on squeaky springs across the ruts and rocked to a halt beside Dave's rental car, red lights blinking with sleepy menace on grimy white roofs. Four pale uniforms stepped out. The men wearing them were young. One was Jerry Orton. They hadn't brought a grappling hook. They used ropes and they weren't good at it. Right away, one of them fell in. He slogged disgustedly back to his car, where he wrapped himself in a blanket and sat hunched up, trading talk with a radio that hissed and crackled.

Under the hulking blackness of the trees, lights went on in one of the campers. A gray woman and a bald man, both in new bathrobes, climbed out and stood close together, watching. From the next camper, a pair of plump young people—long-tailed plaid flannel shirts, lard-white legs—came out, peered with pinched, unbelieving faces at the shouts and movement in the headlight glare on the point, and went back inside. A small dog bolted out of the third camper, streaked across the open ground, yapped hard at the uniforms, and turned and scooted for the camper again with its ears laid back. A woman's voice said, "Bad dog!" and a tinny door slammed.

They emptied the water out of Smith but it didn't help. He lay on his back now in the weeds, roped under the shoulders, his bones showing sharp through the wet, white suit. His teeth were lost. His jaw wouldn't hold his mouth closed. His mouth was a soft black hole. His wet white hair lay all but transparent on the delicate skull. Next to it, one of the uniforms set down an almost empty vodka bottle. Dave stood out of the way as he'd been ordered to, back by the rental car. Cecil sat on the fender and shivered in a thin yellow windbreaker. And suddenly the bald man in the new bathrobe was with them.

"He was always drunk," he said. "Staggering around out here singing all night. Wife and me couldn't sleep."

"Look at it this way," Dave said. "Neither could he."

Cecil said, "Tired of starting over?"

"He had talent," Dave said, "and no one noticed."

"Not for singing," the bald man said and walked off.

A car arrived that was not like the police cars. It was wide and new and hardly made a sound. It was a Mark V painted dark metallic gold. A man in a white Stetson got out of it with a doctor's bag. He wore big wire-frame glasses and bushy sideburns. His Levi's were saddle-worn and his cowboy boots were clotted with manure and straw. He knelt by what was left of Smith. After a busy minute, he said something to Jerry Orton that made both of them laugh. Orton walked around the big car and opened the trunk. The man in the Stetson picked Smith up as if he were sticks and straw and carried him to the trunk and laid him in it. He slammed down the lid. The wind had picked up. Whatever he shouted as he got into the car was blown away. The broad back of the car had many red lights. They winked out one by one among the trees. The wet boy kept battling the static on his radio. One of the dry ones coiled the ropes, levered up the bent lids of the patrol-car trunks, and dropped the ropes inside. The third boy climbed into the trailer and used a flashlight.

Jerry Orton came to Dave. He seemed to do fine without sleep. His childlike blue eyes were clear, his shave was close, every short golden hair on his head was in place. His uniform was crisp. "I want an explanation," he said.

"Years ago," Dave said, "a friend called me at night. I went back to sleep. When I got to his place next morning, he was lying in a bathtub and all of his blood was in the water."

"Not about Smith," Orton said. "He got drunk and fell off there. And he wasn't a friend of yours. His kind don't have friends. I don't care about him. Crazy old drunks are always dying on the beach. I care about my wife and mother and sister." Orton looked at Cecil. "Okay, kid, the excitement's over. You can go now."

Cecil looked at Dave. Dave nodded an eighth of an inch. Cecil slid down off the fender, got behind the wheel of the rental car, started the little motor, backed the car in a half circle, and drove it away through the trees.

Orton said, "Does Medallion Life Insurance Company know you're out of your mind?"

"You can ask them tomorrow at nine," Dave said.

"Because," Orton said, "the things you told my wife tonight are insane. My father prowling around in hippie clothes and dark glasses with marijuana in his pocket, for God's sake! My sister running away with a jigaboo convict, pretending to be kidnapped. A ransom note in my father's closet. My sister's brand-new car down in a ravine."

"Have you looked in that closet?" Dave asked.

"Frances phoned my mother. She looked. There's nothing in there but my father's uniforms and two suits."

Dave listened to the sea splash on the rocks.

"My father wouldn't wear out shoe leather hunting for a man just released from Soledad. He'd go through channels. I've had the department phoning Lester Green's parole officer. Last I heard, he wasn't home, but we'll keep trying."

"George Anderson," Dave said. "He'll tell you Lester is at his mother's place. That's what he told your father, and your father went there looking for Lester."

"Is that what Mrs. Green said?" Orton asked disgustedly. "Because if she did, I know exactly why. It was what you wanted to hear. That's how she is. A very old-fashioned black lady. 'Don't cross the white man boss.' You leaned on her—don't say you didn't."

"What about the marriage license?" Dave asked.

"My father's got friends on the Sacramento force," Orton said. "One of them will check the state records tomorrow. But I can tell you now—there won't be one. It's all in your mind. Why would she want to marry Lester Green?"

"To spite your father," Dave said.

Orton barked a laugh. "You don't know Lester. I've known him since he was four years old. He was scared of his own shadow then. He never changed. He knew how my father felt about blacks. I don't care what Anita would do. Lester Green wouldn't."

"Then why did he end up in jail?"

"He was caught with a stash," Orton said.

"What's Anita's car doing by his mother's house? It's finals week. Why isn't she at college?"

"We went and looked in that ravine," Orton said. "There's nothing down there but wild cucumber vines." Orton squinted at Dave. "Did you really think you could get away with this kind of harassment? Is Medallion that tight for money?"

"You had to drag that car out with a wrecker," Dave said. "Unless you know of an auto-parts supplier open all night. The distributor head for that car is in my motel room. I not only have a witness that the car was in the ravine this afternoon, this whole area saw it there on the late news. And heard it was registered to your father."

"Pictures can be faked." There was a sharp cry. A gull swooped close to their heads. It beat its wings for a second in the glare of the patrol-car headlights, then vanished in the dark. "So you've got Daisy Flynn in your pocket. What else is new? You're male and you're trying to smear Ben Orton. Naturally, she'd go for that. Believe me, viewers aren't going to take it seriously. Wait here." Orton walked to the car where the radio was squawking. He spoke to the boy wrapped in the blanket. The boy rolled up the window. Orton came back.

Dave said, "Your mother drove by Ophelia Green's house this afternoon. When she saw me, she hurried off. Why?"

"Ophelia Green doesn't have a telephone. My mother's housekeeper is sick. Ophelia worked for us years ago. Mom thought she might be willing to help out a few days." Orton snorted. "Sure she hurried off. She'd had enough of you."

"Your father wore those hippie clothes," Dave said. "To the natural-foods place. He offered that pouch of marijuana to anybody who could lead him to Lester Green."

"Don't believe those freaks. They hated my father."

"He didn't burn down the underground paper to keep Eddie Suchak from printing the truth about what happened to Lester Green and why?"

"Be glad nobody else heard you say that," Orton said. "And listen to me and listen to me good. My father was the law in this town. My father would never break the law. No matter what it cost him personally. You wouldn't be able to understand this but I'm going to tell it to you anyway—Ben Orton was an honest man, decent and upright and moral. And that was how he raised me and that's why you make me sick."

"While you were up in that canyon with your wrecker," Dave said, "did you happen to stop in at Mrs. Green's and have a chat with Anita and Lester? I left word with your wife that I thought that might be a nice idea."

"They're not there," Orton said.

"What about magazines?" Dave asked. "With words clipped out of them to make up an authentic-looking kidnap ransom note just like on TV?"

"I told you—Ophelia Green is an old-fashioned black lady. She can't read. What would she want with magazines?"

"Didn't your father tell you," Dave asked, "tampering with evidence is wrong? Wrecking motel rooms? Slashing tires?"

"What the hell are you talking about?"

"I can produce film of one of your officers slashing the tires of my car. Early this afternoon. At the Bayfront Motel. He was wearing shades but I think it was the one in the trailer."

Orton turned and shouted "Thomson" into the dark.

The boy with the flashlight appeared in the doorway of the trailer. Orton motioned to him. He came down the bent steps, shut the trailer door, and crossed the rough ground. "Jesus, what a pigpen," he said. "There's no point in going through that junk. Just shovel it out, is all."

"Would you explain to this man about those slashed tires this afternoon? He owns the car."

"You should have reported that, sir," Thomson said gravely. "I was sure you would or I'd have looked you up right then. What happened was, I saw someone acting suspicious in the motel garage. I parked my car and got out

128

to investigate. He saw me coming and ran. I chased him and lost him. I went back to the car where I'd seen him. I inspected it for damage or signs of attempted break-in."

"What make of car was it?" Orton asked.

"A new Electra. Silver. The tires were slashed. I took the license number. I filed a report."

"I believe every word," Dave said.

Thomson struggled to keep a straight face. "Is that all?" he asked Orton. Orton said it was, and Thomson grinned at Dave the way he'd grinned from his patrol car that afternoon and went back to the trailer. Orton turned to Dave.

"I told you this morning," he said, "your only business in La Caleta was to get my mother her insurance check."

"I can't do that," Dave said. "Not if she conspired in your father's death, and I think she did."

"You broke into her house. I can lock you up for that."

"You can't prove it," Dave said.

"You can sit in jail a long time while I try," Orton said. "Only I don't want you in jail. I don't want you anyplace around here. Where I want you is back in Los Angeles. You go now, tonight. If you don't you're going to hate yourself in the morning."

"Goodbye," Dave said, and walked toward the trees.

The plastic glasses of wine glinted dimly on the pale rectangle of the chest under the splintered mirror. So did the wine bottle. So did the drop-jeweled glass that had held the water with which he'd washed down the pills. The torn loaf of bread squatted there on its flattened paper sack. But the manila envelope with the retouched photo of Ben Orton was gone. And so was the Gremlin distributor head. From the closet, where curved fragments of the broken lamp base lay white and sharp in the dark, Dave took his suitcase, opened it on the tousled bed, and began to empty the drawer where Cecil had neatly folded his clothes.

"I hope," he said, "you weren't planning on entering the film you took today in the Cannes festival. Because I don't think it's going to be around even long enough for a reshowing on the morning news."

Cecil brought Dave's shaving kit from the bathroom. "If you expect me to ask you what you're talking about, forget it." He laid the kit on the bed and got the suit from the closet where he'd hung it. "Where you going?"

"If you'll drive," Dave said, "to Los Angeles."

"Whither thou goest," Cecil said, "there go I."

"It will be boring," Dave said. "I'll be asleep."

"It won't be boring when you wake up," Cecil said.

14

The streetlights died as they drove up Robertson. To the north, hills bulked dark against a smudgy sky. In the empty parking lot, Dave unfolded stiffly from the cramped back seat and crawled out of the little car. The air was cool and moist. There was a hush. Cecil wore black and yellow wet-look shoes with two-inch heels. The noise of the heels echoed off the shopfronts. Garden furniture for sale waited behind wrought-iron fences. Chiffoniers loomed in dusky show windows. A huddle of Victorian dolls in a bowed-glass cabinet blankly witnessed their thirty-thousandth dawn.

Here were the tall, carved doors of Doug Sawyer's gallery. Cecil stopped in front of the arched window and gazed at the single painting there, a portrait of Dave. Dave went to the building corner and turned a key in a door. He led Cecil up narrow, walled stairs that he hated, to the yawning, half-furnished rooms over the gallery. His bedroom had French doors that opened on a roof deck jungly with large tropical plants. The room was wide, long, high ceilinged. The bare floor was cold when they stripped and fell into the bed he'd bought big to try to fill up some of the emptiness.

When the sun came through the French doors it came hot and woke him. Cecil lay far off at the edge of the mattress, face down, an arm hanging limp to the floor. Dave left the bed quietly. He wanted the bathroom. But when he opened the door, there were perfumed steam and Christian Jacques in skimpy red underpants. He stood at the washbasin. Shaving cream was on his face. The hand that held the razor stopped moving. He looked at Dave in the foggy mirror. "Good morning," he said.

"Excuse me." Dave shut the door and went to his room again. Cecil had rolled onto his back. One long, lean, black leg was out of the sheets. Dave sat on the edge of the bed, picked up the phone from the floor, and dialed the hospital. When Amanda came on, he said, "I'm back in L.A. The doctor was waiting for morning. Did Dad wait too?"

"He's fine," she said. "I mean, not fine, but they're letting him out of intensive care. He's over the worst part. He's going to get better, Dave." She made a thin sound that wasn't words. "God—isn't this a hell of a time to cry?"

"It's better than most," Dave said. "I want to be there but I don't know how soon I can make it."

"I'll wait for you," she said. "We both will."

"I hope so," Dave said, and hung up. When he'd undressed, he'd dropped wallet, keys, change, cigarettes, lighter, by the phone. He looked at his watch. He lit a cigarette. Behind him, Cecil made a small, protesting noise. The bed moved. Dave half turned. The sun had beaten on the boy as he slept. He was shiny with sweat. He blinked at Dave, smiled a little, ran a lazy fingertip down Dave's ribs. "Go back to sleep," Dave told him. "You've hardly started."

"You want me to find that woman," Cecil said.

"It's too early yet," Dave said. "When you're ready, help yourself to a shower and breakfast. I'll leave the car. Key's right here. And a key to this place." He worked them off their clips. "Do you need money?"

"No." Cecil's eyes fell shut. "Give us a kiss."

Dave kissed him. Cecil smiled satisfaction and rolled over again. "Thelma Green," he said into the pillow. "Registered nurse. Find her home address. Go see it but don't be conspicuous. Look around for a new lavender Montego." He recited the license number.

"Or a red Kawasaki." Dave patted the hard bump in the sheet made by Cecil's butt. He went to the closet for a short terrycloth robe. "Sleep well," he said, and followed coffee smells down awkward halls to the kitchen. Doug was already dressed, complete with tie. He was laying bacon strips in a skillet. "Add three more, please," Dave said.

Doug turned. "What did you do—drive all night?"

"I can meet those appointments for you at the pet shop," Dave said, "while you take her to the rest home."

"Everything's sold," Doug said. "Only truck drivers will be coming today. The bike-shop man will let them in. What about your father?"

"It looks like he may make it," Dave said. "I didn't drive. I slept. Somebody else drove. Now he's sleeping."

Jacques came into the kitchen in a jumpsuit of crushed gold velvet open to the navel. A thin gold chain was around his smooth, brown throat. His feet were in sandals. They were handsome feet but he looked wrong without an armload of menus. He said to Dave, "You have a new lover?"

133

"A chauffeur." Doug opened the fridge, put in the bacon package, and took out a box of eggs. "Dave is monogamous." The toaster bell said *ding.* "Aren't you, Dave?"

"Monogamous?" Jacques took a papaya from a basket, a knife from a drawer, sliced the papaya in two. "Has that to do with black people?"

"Not quite yet," Dave said.

He went back to the bathroom. He showered quickly. He'd shave later. He wanted to sit out there under the rubber trees with them at breakfast. Not to make them uncomfortable. To see how uncomfortable it would make him. Yesterday morning he'd have bet he already knew. Cecil asleep now in his bed suggested he could still surprise himself. Did that ever stop?

Carl Brandstetter wore new blue pajamas, but this time the color let him down. It made his eyes look faded, and accented the bad blue color of his mouth. Against the hospital pillows and sheets he looked leached out. The silver sheen was gone from his hair—it was just white and old now. A razor had nicked his jawline. He'd never have done that to himself. He had the voice that actors give board chairmen of multimillion-dollar corporations. And managing directors. He was both. But this morning his voice wasn't like that. The force had gone out of it.

He said, "If Mrs. Orton covered up for those kids, and then young what's-his-name, Jerry, covered up for her— Medallion's off the hook."

"If we can prove it." Dave leaned on the foot of the bed next to a little color TV mounted there. He was gloomy. "But that ransom note is ashes now."

"You booted that," his father said.

"You were dying," Dave said. "It distracted me."

"Excuses, excuses," his father said.

"Carl!" Amanda stood beside the bed in a mock 1927 dress, raspberry color, sash around the hips, loops of long beads, very short skirt. "Dave was with you all night after your attack. He never slept. Then he drove halfway to San Francisco. If he made a mistake—"

"Take it easy," Carl Brandstetter said. "He doesn't make mistakes—not the kind he can't straighten out. But if I didn't criticize, he'd think I was sick." He worked up a smile for Dave. It wasn't the old mocking grin but it was meant to be. "Forget about the ransom note," he said. "You aren't licensed to steal. Breaking and entering was bad enough. Young Orton was right about that. You don't need the note. Not if you can find those kids."

"I'm working on it," Dave said, "but it's a long shot."

"You've made those before," his father said.

Across the sunny room, Doug, neat in his suit and tie, leaned on the sill with his back to the wide window that showed the tops of locust trees dense with yellow blossom. He divided his attention between his shoetops and his watch. He said, "Those are the only kind he likes. Two hundred fifty miles or more." His look at Dave was brief and bleak.

Dave said to his father, "This is a big city to cover alone. I can't get police help. L.A. won't move unless La Caleta asks them to. And La Caleta isn't about to ask."

"Do they think you've left for good up there?"

"My car's still at the motel," Dave said, "and I didn't check out of my room. That may bother them enough to give me time. But once they send for them, those kids won't open their mouths. We can bring on ten lawyers. The district attorney there belongs to the Ortons—which means the grand jury. No one in Madrone County is going to indict an Orton for anything."

Amanda said, "But it was an Orton who was killed."

"And they've got a suspect they can't wait to hang. The dead man's own blue-eyed little girl? Never."

"Insular," Carl Brandstetter said. "I met them, years ago. Homer Nowell and that bunch. When I was married to Helena. We dragged a two-horse trailer all the way to Sangre de Cristo for some palomino show. Ranchers, growers, Cadillacs, Cessnas, five-hundred-dollar cowboy boots. They can get ugly with each other about who has the most silver mounting on a saddle, but I'd judge that if anything threatened any one of them, they'd close ranks."

"Was that where we went?" Dave said.

"That's right—you were along. Insisted on stopping to look at the fish cannery. Helena didn't like it. Didn't like much that wasn't a horse. She called you The Colt. I'd forgotten that."

Dave grinned. "I wondered if she called you Stallion."

Carl Brandstetter snorted. "She called me a lot of things toward the end. But never Stallion. No." Alarm widened his eyes suddenly and he began groping frantically at the side of the bed. Dave knew what for—the oxygen tube he'd torn off when the nurse had left. Now the nurse was back, stout and angry.

"This has gone on far too long," she snapped. "Mrs. Brandstetter, I'm surprised at you." She fished up the waxy tube and taped it firmly across Carl Brandstetter's upper lip. "This is a sick man with a very tired heart." She glared at Amanda, at Dave, even at Doug. "Out, please."

Dave touched his father's shoulder. His father caught his wrist, pulled him close. "A thermos of martinis," he hissed, "and a carton of Benson Hedges."

136

"And in case those don't do it," Dave asked, "a gun?"

"You wouldn't refuse a dying man's last request."

"Only to keep him alive." Dave went to the door the nurse was holding open. She was Japanese and her scowl made her look like a demon guarding a Kyoto temple. Amanda and Doug were already in the hall.

"Don't do anything reckless," Carl Brandstetter said. "It's only money, you know. Go carefully with that black boy."

"What?" Dave turned. "Who?"

"The one who killed Orton. Green, isn't it?"

"Oh—that black boy," Dave said. "I will."

A wire-mesh fence flared with wine-bright bougainvillea outside one window. Outside the other, a wisteria vine with a twisted trunk thick as a tree's shaded a patio. On one of the room's white walls, Doug had hung a big color plate of dogs of the world that used to hang in Sawyer's Pet Shop. He'd given it a new frame and a new glass. Curtains, bed-spread, carpet, the covers on the chairs, were cheerful oranges and yellows. The room still looked institutional. In a new cotton print dress and a white button sweater, Belle Sawyer stood small by the door and blinked at the room through a thick lens with her one bright eye. The other lens was pasted over with cloth. She'd lost an eye to a hawk's claw years ago. Her hair had always been frizzy. Today it was neatly set and that added to the strangeness. The thing that took away from the strangeness a little was that she held a cage with birds in it—two small green parrots with rosy faces and blue rumps. They shrieked and whistled. She looked at Doug and Dave over the cage and said:

"I do have my rational times, you know. When I know

who I am and where I am. I'm not going to like this place. I want my animals."

Doug took the cage from her. "I don't like it any better than you do." He set the cage by a window. "But it was the only place where they'd even let the birds in."

"Never mind," she said. "They're lively."

Doug gazed out the window. "You can see the hills."

" 'I will lift up mine eyes,' " she said.

The stout woman with brassy hair who ran the place came out of her office as they passed. "I hope the other guests don't complain," she said. "Those birds are terribly noisy." Inside the office in back of her were artificial flowers and a big artificial portrait of Jesus. Doug looked at it and then up at the hot blue sky. A mockingbird shouted from a television antenna. In the ferny leafage of the wisteria a gang of sparrows quarreled. Doug said to the woman, "Just like the ones out here." He gave her a smile and turned for the patio entryway. "They're praising God," he said. In the car he twisted the ignition key and revved the engine angrily. "There's an instinct in people. Barnyard. One of them begins to bleed, they can't wait to attack it." He kicked the brake and jerked the car into traffic. "God damn it—I should have closed the gallery and kept the pet shop running. For her. Till she dies."

"This can drag on for years," Dave said. "The doctor told you. She knows it. She wouldn't let you."

"How could she stop me?" Doug drove two blocks in grim silence and stopped for a light. Shrill little kids in bright colors swarmed over the blacktop of the school playground. Doug said, "The gallery's nothing but a faggot game. Even if it was making money. The pet shop was her life." The signal light changed to green and he swung the car sharply down a side street.

"Where are you going?" Dave asked.

"Back to get her out of there," Doug said.

"The pet shop's gone," Dave said. "So is the house—remember? Look, Doug, this is old age, illness. Nothing you can fight—not and win. In this kind of bind there are no heroes, no villains. There are only victims."

"Oh, shut up," Doug said dully.

"You haven't seen many endings," Dave said. "In my line of work I've seen hundreds. They're never neat. That place looks decent. It's nearby. You can visit her."

"I'll be the only one," Doug said. "A shop like that—your friends come during business hours. Friends? They've already forgotten her." He glanced at Dave. There were tears in his eyes. "You're a sententious jerk. There are too villains. And I don't like the role."

"Don't accept it," Dave said. "It's miscasting."

Doug dodged a bicycle. "And what I hate about it most is that tomorrow I won't hate it as much. And next week or next month, I'll hardly remember." He was crying now.

"Pull over," Dave said. "I'll drive."

When they reached the parking lot on Robertson it was nearly full. The rental car was there—still or again. Dave checked his watch. Ten past noon. He walked with Doug up the street past shops now open for business, with peacock chairs, knitted afghans, Franklin stoves set out on the sidewalks in the sun. Music drifted from an open door.

Doug asked, "What kind of pre-Columbian figures?"

"West coast," Dave said. "Colima, Jalisco, Nayarit. Classic period. The Nayarit are the deformed ones—right? Hunchbacks, women with misshapen skulls?"

"Terra-cottas," Doug said. "Polychrome finish?"

Across the street, a miniature brown youth wrapped in a long white apron sloshed water from a bucket across the sidewalk in front of The Bamboo Raft and used a push broom to sweep last night's stains into the gutter.

"Big ones," Dave said. "Glossy."

Doug pushed his key into the blue door. He was shaking his head. "In La Caleta, of all places." The door opened and his voice echoed up the stairs. "A new gallery, you said. Who's their backer? What millionaire?"

"They is a woman." Dave followed Doug up the stairs. "It's more than a business arrangement. Her backer is the local police chief. Was."

"The murdered one? You didn't say he was wealthy."

"He wasn't. He worked for a living."

Doug's short laugh was sharp on the narrow stairs. "No wonder he's dead. Dave, we're talking about tens of thousands of dollars. He must have been crooked as hell." They reached the top step. "Mexico won't let them out of the country anymore. And there just aren't that many floating around loose." Faint sounds of guitar and bongo drifted from the big hollow room where the stereo equipment sat on bare flooring. An old Cal Tjader album. Dave didn't look in there. He followed Doug to the sun-bright kitchen. Doug said, "Museums hang on to the ones they're lucky enough to own." He dropped ice cubes into a tall glass.

"I think it's museums she's selling to," Dave said.

Doug dumped vodka over the ice. "Not many private collectors have that kind of money."

"The one who unloaded this batch has—now."

Doug made a skeptical noise. "It was a damn secret transaction." He brought a pitcher of tomato juice from the fridge. "You know how hard I've been looking. There was no announcement, catalogue, auction—not even any gossip."

"Look no farther," Dave said. "Drive up there."

"With whose life savings?" Doug poured tomato juice after the vodka and set the pitcher back.

"Maybe there's one with a chip out of it," Dave said. "Isn't it early to start boozing? You already cried."

Doug tilted Worcestershire sauce into the glass, spun the ice cubes with a finger, kept his back to Dave. "Right. This was in case you started talking about us."

"What is there left to say?" Dave asked.

Doug turned around. "You really don't give a damn, do you? About Christian—walking in, finding him here?"

"And before him, Kovaks," Dave said. "And before him the mechanic from European Motors. I used to think you only did it to get my attention. I don't think so anymore."

"Maybe I gave up," Doug said.

"There was no call to start," Dave said.

Heels knocked in the hall and Cecil came in. "I found her," he said. The sunlight made the yellow pants and jacket shine. "Like you said—nothing to it. Phoned the State Board of Nursing and stepped in the car. She isn't even far away. Few miles south, down that next big street —La Cienega?"

"Doug Sawyer," Dave said, "Cecil Harris." He watched them shake hands, Doug sulky, Cecil wary. Dave asked, "What's it like? The car there? The motorcycle?"

"Apartment buildings set in a park—trees, lawns, flower beds. Black now but it hasn't been black long. Streets where CHITTERLINGS in a market window still looks wrong. Her type—when it gets so people know it's a black neighborhood, they move on out." He gave Dave a sly smile. "You never thought I'd be conspicuous. No way."

Dave grinned. "Feel used, do you?"

Cecil laughed. The far-off record was still playing. He snapped his fingers to the beat. Shoulders and hips twisting, he crossed the kitchen to the open roof-deck doors. "I felt so inconspicuous among all those darling pickaninnies off to school on their fifty-dollar skateboards, I went right up and rang the lady's doorbell."

"I'll be in the gallery," Doug said, and left.

Cecil blinked. "He can't be jealous. What about the island queen?"

Dave listened cheerlessly to the clatter of Doug's heels down the stairs. "Don't worry your pretty head," he said. "You can't tell the players without a program. What did Thelma Green say?"

"She was dressed up in her nurse outfit and she had her coat over her arm, about to go to work. I said Lester was a friend of mine from school, told me to look him up. She said she didn't know anything about it. He wasn't there. But I saw a duffel bag on the floor just inside the door, and she is definitely not the kind of lady that would travel with a duffel bag."

"So you waited until she left and went back?"

"They've got this security guard so old all that holds him up is the starch in his uniform, but he kept after me like I was about to rip off every TV in the place. I went back to the car, drove up and down streets. Waste of my time and your gas. The Kawasaki was how they got down here to L.A. all right—but it wasn't where I could find it."

"Then how do you know?" Dave said. "Where is it?"

"I got thirsty," Cecil said. "Stopped at the local liquor store for a Coke. Lots of excitement. Seems the place got knocked over last night. Black boy with a beard and a fat girl with long blond hair. They had a little snub-nose police revolver, you know? Everybody on the floor, all that? They cleaned out the cash drawer and ran for their little red motorcycle, but right then a black and white just happened to come around the corner. So—I guess where we find it now is the police garage, right?"

15

The small green room had a wide window. Outside it, up-right green steel slats sliced the sunlight that beat in. It was hot and the cold air that fell from a ceiling grille was no match for it. A uniformed officer took handcuffs off the wrists of a frail-looking black boy in a beard and a fake leather jacket. The officer left the room, pulling the door shut after him. The boy sat on a green steel chair at a green steel table where someone had left a stained and crumpled paper napkin, a half cup of curdled white coffee, and the bones of a supermarket barbecued chicken in a throwaway tin pan. The boy tried to see Dave against the window glare but gave up and looked at the man seated across from him at the table. The man had a broken nose and shoulders that strained the fabric of his shirt. His collar was unbuttoned, the knot of his tie dragged down. His eyes were bloodshot, and he needed a shave. He was Lieutenant Ken Barker of the LAPD. He said:

"This is not about the liquor-store holdup."

The boy tried to see Dave again. "No? Why not?"

"It's about kidnapping, extortion, and murder."

"No way." The boy stood up and lunged for the door. Barker caught him, rammed a knee into his butt, flattened him against the wall, twisted his arms up behind his back. The boy struggled. "No way," he said again. "I know what this is. You got some monster case you can't solve and then some dumb spook kid tries a little two-bit stickup and you got an instant candidate for death row. Well, not me. No way, man, no way."

"Every which way," Barker said. "Starting with who you are and where you come from. You didn't do yourself any good not telling us. The license on your bike told us."

"Yeah? What does it mean?" Lester said.

"It means you're not just some dumb spook kid." Barker spun the boy and hoisted him like a big, awkward puppet back to his chair. "You are a very special dumb spook kid." He set him down hard. "This man will explain to you why."

Dave said, "Two years ago, you and the girl you were arrested with last night applied for a marriage license, and right away you were busted for possession of marijuana and convicted and sent to Soledad. It was a setup and you knew it and you knew who did it to you."

"I never said so," Lester said.

"You were afraid something worse would happen," Dave said. "To you. To the girl. It's no special shame. Everybody was afraid of him."

"I want a lawyer," Lester Green said.

"You don't need a lawyer to listen," Barker said.

Dave said, "On the sixteenth of this month you were let out of Soledad. You reported to your parole officer. In a new green Gremlin driven by the same girl. The one whose

145

father had you locked up. Next day, he got a note demanding twenty-five thousand dollars for the safe return of his daughter. And the day after that, he was murdered."

Barker sat down and said, "Try that on your paranoia."

"I don't have to say anything." Lester eyed the cigarette pack Dave held out. He took a cigarette and let Dave light it for him. "I'm a law student. I know my rights."

"You also knew this man was after you," Barker said. "You heard your mother tell him about her sister-in-law here in Los Angeles. Yet when you ran, you ran straight to her."

"For money," Dave said. "Mrs. Orton didn't have any. Her late husband had spent it on a pretty lady and her art gallery. Jerry Orton's wife buys cameras and lenses that would bankrupt a rock star. Lester's mother hasn't a dime. But Aunt Thelma smelled trouble and didn't want any part of it."

Lester stared at Dave like a little kid watching a magician take silver dollars out of his ears.

"That makes it bright," Barker asked, "to then go out and knock over a liquor store practically next door?"

"It wasn't his idea," Dave said. "It was Anita's. She wanted to go home. She was tired of the game. All that had kept her in it, in La Caleta, was Lester's mother. All that made her run to L.A. was her brother. He told her to disappear for a while."

"Is she all right?" Lester said.

"She'll always be all right," Dave told him.

Barker said, "As soon as she learned that we knew her identity, she phoned home, crying."

"Her mother is on her way down here," Dave said, "to bail her out. Not you. Her."

"I didn't write any note," Lester said.

146

"It wasn't written," Barker said. "The words were clipped from a magazine and pasted on a sheet of paper."

Dave said, "I found the magazine yesterday, in your mother's house. You know that. You were there."

"Show me." Lester acted scornful. "You don't have any magazine. You don't have any note."

"I don't need them," Dave said. "I have you."

"Why? The one who killed Orton is in jail."

"You don't think so," Barker said.

"Don't tell me what I think," Lester said.

"The lieutenant is right." Dave drew out a chair and sat next to Lester. The jacket with its zippers and bright little chains gave off a chemical smell. "It's what you and I have in common. Neither of us thinks that man did it."

"She didn't tell you that," Lester said.

"She didn't have to," Barker said. "You hid. You ran away. Mr. Brandstetter here didn't have any ransom note, he didn't have any magazine—so what were you afraid of?"

"I don't have to say anything." Lester stood up.

"That's right, you don't," Barker said. "The answer is obvious. You killed him. Sit down."

Lester went to the door. "I want to go back to my cell. I didn't kill him. But even if I did, it's none of your business. It happened in La Caleta. And the La Caleta police— they're never going to send for me." He gave Dave a crooked smile. "You know that."

"If it was up to them," Dave said. "It's not. It's up to me. If the wrong man is convicted of that murder, my company drops seventy-five thousand dollars. I'm not going to let that happen."

On the street below, a police siren moaned.

Lester Green said, "How can you stop it? Shit, man, they ran you out of town."

"I left to find you," Dave said. "No. Medallion Life is a big, powerful company, Lester. It hires big, powerful lawyers. All the La Caleta district attorney has against Cliff Kerlee is one piece of very suspect evidence. It was good enough for a grand jury consisting of the dead man's friends. But a real lawyer will shred that case in a day when it comes to trial. I'm sending a real lawyer."

"And then its my turn?" Lester said.

"That grand jury will never indict Anita Orton," Dave said. "Figure it out. Who does that leave?"

"You," Barker said. "All alone."

"No way." Lester yanked open the door. The uniformed officer looked at him from the hallway. He had soft brown Mexican eyes and a neat mustache. He closed a fist around the handle of his nightstick. Lester let the door fall shut. When he turned back there was a gray cast to his skin. "How is that going to save your seventy-five thousand dollars?"

"Anita was with you all the way," Dave said. "That will come out at your trial if you never say a word."

"She wasn't due any insurance," Lester said. "He wrote her off. When he found out about her and me."

"But after he was dead," Dave said, "her mother helped keep you hidden. Her brother destroyed evidence linking you to the murder. And helped you escape arrest. They were due insurance. No, they won't lose out for murder. They'll lose out for conspiracy to obstruct justice and to defraud an insurance company. And our only way to them is to nail you for the murder."

Lester stared at him. He licked his lips. He moved his head from side to side. His voice came hollow. "No. I didn't do it, man." The hands he held out were shaking. "You've got to believe me. I didn't kill him. He was already dead when I got there."

Barker bowed his head and rubbed his flattened nose to hide a smile. He rose and took the thin arm in the honcho jacket and led Lester back to the chair next to Dave's. The boy dropped onto it as if his knees had given out. Barker went back to the door, poked his head into the hall, and said something. He closed the door. "We'll have coffee in a minute," he said. "What passes for coffee around here." He sat down. "So you did go there. By appointment—right? To collect the money."

"No." Lester's hands lay on the table. He stared at them. But he plainly didn't see them, didn't even feel them. The cigarette had burned down between his fingers. Dave took the smoldering butt and rubbed it out in the little pan of chicken bones. The coal hissed in the grease. Lester said softly, "I went there to apologize."

Barker made a disgusted sound. "You went there for twenty-five big bills and instead he pulled a gun and said he was going to send your black ass back to prison and you smashed his head in and ran away with the gun. It was a police gun you used in your hit on the liquor store."

"I took the gun," Lester said. "But he was already dead. Laying there with his head in a puddle of blood. It wasn't any gun did that. His skull was busted in."

Shadows of pigeons flickered across the sunlit window slats. "Your mother sent you, didn't she?" Dave said. "When she found out about the note. You'd do what she told you but Anita wouldn't and she didn't go."

"It was a joke to her," Lester said. "Laughs, you know? To me too. I mean, sort of." He moved his shoulders. "Well, maybe not a joke, exactly."

"Not exactly," Barker said dryly.

149

"We knew he'd guess where the note came from," Lester said. "Who sent it and what for. Oh, we wanted the bread, all right. But we never thought he'd pay it for any fake kidnapping. He'd pay it to keep us from making him look like a fool to everybody. To shut us up, get rid of us."

"Your mother didn't think it was a joke," Dave said.

"We told her we wanted to hide there because we'd gotten married and couldn't figure out how to tell him."

"I wondered why she let you sleep together."

"Then he came looking for me, told her about the note, and soon as he left she was after me with a broom." A small-boy smile twitched the corner of his mouth. "You better believe it. She never quits. Something evil—she keeps hitting it. I was to crawl to Ben Orton on my knees and confess to him with tears in my eyes and beg him to forgive me." Lester whispered a wry laugh. "That's how she said. How she saw it. Like some corny old movie."

"But you went," Dave said.

"She was right," Lester said. "Look at me now."

"This isn't bad," Barker said. "It can get a whole hell of a lot worse." A shoe tapped the door. He got up to open the door. "And it probably will." A black officer in uniform handed him a plastic tray with big paper cups of coffee steaming on it. Barker set the tray on the table. "Because when you found that body you didn't step to the telephone and call the police."

"Oh, man." Lester closed his eyes and wagged his head. He opened his eyes wide. "The police was who set me up with that dope under my fender." He tapped the tabletop with a strict finger. "They knew I knew that. How they'd think was—who had better reason to kill him? No, I didn't call any police. I got the hell out of there."

"And hid." Barker set one of the paper cups in front of

150

him. "Which makes sense." He set a second cup in front of Dave. "What doesn't make sense is that you kept hiding." He set down his own cup and tilted the tray. Candy-stripe plastic stir sticks slid off it onto the tabletop with a delicate rattle, along with paper napkins and packets of sugar and powdered cream. He set the tray on the floor. "They made an arrest. They got an indictment. You had to hear about that."

"They weren't looking for anyone else," Dave said. "They thought they had Cliff Kerlee dead to rights. Why didn't you come out?"

Lester stirred his coffee. He blew at the steam. He said flatly, "Because I knew he didn't do it."

Barker tipped his coffee over. It spread hot across the table and splashed into his lap. He yelped and jumped to his feet. He grabbed up paper napkins and mopped himself. "What the hell do you mean?"

"I mean," Lester said slowly and exactly, "I saw that body. I searched through the pockets of that body for that stupid note. I'm going to see that body in my mind for the rest of my life. And there was no tote bag by that body. No tote bag anyplace around there."

"Ho," Dave said softly.

"I'm into law—was," Lester said. "And nobody had to tell me the case was shaky. He had a witness. All they had was planted evidence. He could get off. I wasn't showing my face till he was convicted."

"They did all right with planted evidence in your case, and any jury they picked would have seen him promise to kill Ben Orton on TV." Barker left off trying to dry his pants, sat down, and slapped the soggy brown wad of paper napkins on the table. "Not good enough, Lester. Tell us the rest."

The boy slumped in the steel chair and looked old. He sighed. "Yeah. Shit. All right." He eyed Barker glumly. "I was seen."

Barker showed smoky teeth.

Lester said, "Like I say, I ran. Slipped in the patio—it was wet. I ran up the hill. Fastest way out of there. Drop down the other side, there's the highway. When I got to the ridge, I looked back. And a woman came out into the patio. It was too soon. No way she didn't see me."

"Has she said so?" Barker asked.

"Why should she?" Lester said. "Police didn't take me. They took Kerlee. But if they ever did take me—"

Dave frowned. "Hold it. What woman? Mrs. Orton?"

Lester shook his head. "It was pretty far and it was starting to get dark, but it wasn't Mrs. Orton. Too tall and thin. She had a manila envelope under her arm. And she was carrying a can, like a gasoline can, you know, only it was black. Anyway, she had red hair."

16

On a Sangre de Cristo side street, an orange rubbish truck opened steel jaws and a youth in orange coveralls heaved bulging green plastic bags of trash between the jaws from a grassy curb. Dave stopped the rental car. In hard late-afternoon sun glare, Cecil blinked at him.

"You don't make it easy not to ask questions."

Dave grinned. "You look great in that hat." It was yellow, with a broad brim tilted up on one side and a fluffy cerise plume. Dave had bought it for him in Los Angeles, not far from the glass police building. Four hours and twenty-eight minutes ago. Dave flicked the brim of the hat with a finger, opened the car door, and got out.

The youth in orange coveralls used a clumsily gloved hand to yank down a lever at the side of the truck. Machinery whined, the steel jaws groaned closed, there was crunching and grinding. The youth gave a shrill whistle, the truck lumbered on, he jogged after it. Dave stepped out quickly and caught a greasy sleeve. "May I ask you a question?"

The boy stopped and tilted his head. "About politics? About products?"

"About these trucks," Dave said. "How many are there? How many of you work them?"

"Two trucks, four of us." The boy was gold skinned, blue eyed, and well spoken. He should have been playing badminton on a private beach in Malibu. "Except sometimes. Like today. Today one of the trucks has its insides all over the garage floor." He checked a watch on a grimy wrist. It was an expensive watch. "Means the two of us have to cover two whole districts. That's why we're out so late."

"When do you study for exams?" Dave asked.

"On my off days," the boy said. "This is a good job. There's a long waiting list for this job. Normally it's only five, six hours, two, three days a week."

From the high cab of the truck another blond youth stuck his head. "Come on, Kevin." The diesel revved impatiently.

Kevin waved a glove. "What did you want to know?"

"Whether you remember picking up a charred gasoline can. About two weeks ago. On Cholla street."

The boy in the truck blasted on its horn.

"I'm coming," Kevin called. "Yeah. Not me—Paul. It had a police-department stencil on it. Didn't look any good anymore but we turned it over to them anyway."

Cecil came up. Dave asked him, "Do you know her exact address?"

"Two forty-one," Cecil said.

"Along there somewhere." The boy frowned. "Who are you?"

"Insurance." Dave stuck a card into a pocket of the orange coveralls. "It's evidence in an arson case."

The diesel horn shouted down the street again. Dogs began to bark. Kevin ran for the next stack of trash.

News, or what Channel Ten chose to see as news, kept happening. It was close to six o'clock. The side room in the cinderblock building on top of the mountain was noisy again with typewriters and teletypes, and foggy with cigarette smoke the gale-force air conditioning couldn't cope with. Telephones rang. Hiked shoulders held receivers to mouths and ears while pencils scribbled on yellow pads. No one paid any attention to Dave and Cecil when they edged their way between the desks. Daisy Flynn was marking copy again with the black felt-tip pen. She didn't see them either—not right away. When she did, she yanked off her glasses and glared at Cecil.

"Where the hell have you been?"

"They stole my film, didn't they?" Cecil said.

"You were supposed to be here at five this morning with an interview tape," she said. "What? Yes—they stole your film." She turned Dave a sour green stare. "They're everywhere, aren't they—the tentacles of a great insurance corporation?" She looked at Cecil again. "What are you doing with him?"

"As Scoop Harris of the Hoof and Mouth Bureau," Cecil said, "nothing. As Cecil Harris, first grader, I'm learning the alphabet. But slowly."

"I don't know what you're jabbering about." She fiddled irritably with her digital watch again. "But you are up to your Afro in trouble around here." She scrambled papers together off the desk. "Naturally, I telephoned your school. They couldn't find you either, which didn't make them

155

happy. They phoned your home in San Francisco." She got to her feet. "Your older brother then got on the horn to me. And if you think I'm overreacting, wait until he gets to you."

"I brought everything back," Cecil said. "Video and audio. They're outside in my van."

"We'll sort you out later," she said. "One torn and bleeding limb at a time. Meanwhile, I have a newscast to do." She started off.

Dave stepped in front of her. "Give your sidekicks a chance for once. You and I need to talk."

She looked him up and down sharply. "What about? You mean I get that interview?" She laid down her script and pulled open a desk drawer. "Channel Ten's Newsdesk learns at last what you're doing in the Ben Orton case and why?"

"You're kidding," Dave said. "You didn't turn Cecil loose on me for Channel Ten's Newsdesk. You turned him loose to keep me from getting my job done."

"I didn't turn him loose." She took her little white cassette recorder out of the drawer. "I simply didn't try to stop him. Why wouldn't I want you to get your job done?"

"That's what we need to talk about," Dave said. "But I don't think you'll want that." He touched the cold little box. "Because the subject isn't going to be my part in the Ben Orton case. It's going to be yours."

She stiffened. "What do you mean?"

"You don't want me to say it here." Dave glanced at the desks that crowded close, the busy staffers at the desks. "Shall we step outdoors?"

"I'm stepping into the studio." She dropped the recorder back and slammed the drawer. She snatched up her script.

156

"You don't know what you're talking about." She walked off.

He went after her. "I'm talking about a fire-blackened gasoline can marked 'La Caleta Police' picked up by the trash collectors around Monday the nineteenth at your address."

She halted. He couldn't tell whether she was pale or not. Her makeup was too thick. But the green eyes that stared at him through a fringe of false lashes were suddenly dull. So was her voice. "Wait a minute," she said, and pushed out the door into the hallway. Cecil looked grave and afraid. Dave gave him a one-cornered smile and watched the red hand of a clock on the wall. It wasn't a minute till she was back. Without script. "Come on," she said.

She came to a stop on the packed open ground beyond the cars that angled in a row against the blank wall of the building, whose gray the dropping sun turned copper color. There was silence. The sky was beginning to go green. The hawk hung in it again, high and almost motionless.

"Now, what's this about?" She tried to be defiant.

"You came out here," Dave said. "You tell me."

"I came out here," she snapped, "because you are talking dangerous nonsense and I want it to stop."

"What was dangerous," Dave said, "was your being at Ben Orton's the day and hour he was killed."

"You're out of your mind." She said it with energy and contempt but her long red nails were digging into her palms. "What would I be doing there?"

"I've got a couple of answers," Dave said, "but I'd rather have them from you."

"I wasn't there," she said. "Who told you I was?"

"You know that," Dave said. "Lester Green."

"Lester—" Her voice failed. She wavered on her legs. A

157

bony hand groped out for support. It was Cecil's arm she found. "But Lester Green is in prison."

"He was out that day," Dave said. "He wanted to see Ben Orton but he got there too late. Orton was dead. Lester lost his head and ran. But at the top of the hill he looked back. And saw you in the patio. With a charred gasoline can in your hand. You know he saw you. You saw him."

She looked away at the shadows gathering in the folds of the hills. She breathed in deeply, shoulders rising and dropping. She turned Dave a weary, defenseless look. She nodded. "I saw him." Her smile was thin and ironic. "I thought he was a workman clearing brush. The way they do when it gets dry like this. Against fires."

"Because he was black," Cecil said. "Well, you're wrong. Around here, it's white middle-class boys get the nigger jobs."

"I forgot." She let go of him, crossed the hardpan on wobbly heels, and leaned back against a very small car. The sun struck into her eyes. She shaded them with a hand. "Do you know," she asked Dave, "who Eddie Suchak was?"

"He published an underground paper in La Caleta," Dave said, "until it got burned out. Which is where the gasoline can fits in—right?"

"I was on vacation that month," she said, "but the police told our crew it was the wiring. His printing equipment was too much for it. The building was old and run down."

"You wrote for him," Dave said.

"Not for long," she answered grimly. "But it did feel nice —freedom." She smiled to herself a second, then squinted up at him. "May I have a cigarette?"

Dave held out his pack. Her hand shook but she managed to slip a cigarette out. Then she dropped it. Cecil picked it up and handed it to her, and Dave lit it for her. The air was still and the smoke hung in it. She said, "I believed it—about the wiring. Until two weeks ago. Two weeks? Yes."

"When Suchak died," Dave said, "in a veterans' hospital up the coast."

"Things go wrong with the kidneys," she said, "when they're confined to wheelchairs. Kidneys? I don't know. Something inside. Unless they get regular therapy. And he wouldn't stay still for it. But it wasn't only that. He was angry all the time. Stupid wars, greedy corporations, corrupt politics—everything out there." She nodded vaguely toward the town below in its bowl of brown hills. "It depends on who you are but he was a very delicate mechanism. Not put together to stand it. And then there was—" She broke off. The fingers of a hanging hand had strayed to the car's license plate and were uselessly tracing the numbers. She looked down at them. Her voice held pity and rage. "He wanted to make love. He couldn't. Which was pathetic, and he couldn't bear being pathetic." She looked up again, tears in her eyes. "It wasn't paralysis that killed him. It was bitterness."

"And you don't think anymore that it was faulty wiring that burned down his paper," Dave said.

"He brought me the can, wrapped in brown paper and tied with twine. And an envelope. Not here. To my apartment. He left them on the service porch. I suppose it was that same night. 'To be opened in the event of my death' —that's what he'd written on them. I didn't know what it meant, why he'd left whatever they were with me. We hadn't spoken in months." She looked at Dave with winter in her face. "I expect you know why. He said he wasn't a man." Her soundless laugh was tender and derisive. "He was ten times the man Ben Orton ever was."

"But he ran from Ben Orton," Dave said.

"Didn't we all?" She shrugged, dropped the cigarette, stepped on it. "Anyway—it was a day or two after he died that I remembered the package and the envelope."

"And in the package," Dave said, "was the gasoline can left behind by whichever of Ben Orton's boys likes to play with matches, so there'd be no mistake in Suchak's mind about who burned him out and why. And in the envelope was a Xerox of the marriage license made out to Anita Orton and Lester Green. Along with Suchak's story of the tie between the license and Lester's arrest."

"And the fire." She nodded. "Written in pencil. His typewriter was at the paper." She sighed, pushed away from the little car, dusted her hands together. "So I took the can and the envelope and a lot of rage, and drove up to Ben Orton's. I was going to put the story on the air but I wanted to confront him with it first. To see his face. Only when I saw it, it was surprised at something else—the last thing that would ever surprise it."

"You went in through the patio," Dave said.

"It was wet," she said. "I had an old habit of going in that way—from years before." Her glance flickered away, flickered back. "And there he lay in his own pig blood with his little pig gun in his hand. I was too angry to be sick. I stood over him and gave the speech I'd worked up on my way there in the car." Her laugh at herself was harsh and despairing. "As if he could hear me dead when he never once heard me alive. I started to leave the study the way I'd come, and the patio gate squeaked. I ran into the bathroom and locked the door. Someone came into the study and I just stood there trembling, praying for them to go away, whoever they were. And they did."

"You should have given him more time," Dave said. "Look—there was a phone there. You knew what to do."

She sucked in her cheeks and shook her head at him. "Not a chance. Louise Orton's deepest longing for twenty-five years has been to punish me. I thought she'd killed him. I still think so. For flaunting that art-gallery woman, Windrow, in her face—bringing her right into La Caleta."

"What about Kerlee? Lester says his tote bag wasn't by the body. You knew that. And you still said nothing."

"That was why I was pleased when you showed up. You might be able to save him. I couldn't. Not without taking his place. I was seen."

"That didn't worry you," Dave said. "That was only some workman burning weeds."

"I don't mean by him," she said. "When I got to the foot of Orton's road in my car, another car was standing there. A 1928 Rolls-Royce, the only one of its kind in this part of the world. Richard T. Nowell's. And he was in it."

17

It waited, almost hidden by big boulders, off the Coast Road. It stood high and erect on its big wheels in grassy sand. Its paint was pearl gray with neat coachwork striping in red. Its hood was nickel plated, without a scratch, without so much as a thumb smudge. It had been cared for every day of its life and showed it. Cecil shook his head in awe.

"How much?" he said.

"Thirty-five thousand," Dave said. "But it isn't happiness. Come on." He followed footprints between tall rocks. He had to use his hands in order to keep upright. Then the width was easy only for children. Dave edged through. Behind him, it sounded as if Cecil were in trouble with his heels. The cove was small. The rocks dropped to a space of sand maybe ten feet square. Richard T. Nowell sat on the sand, his back against a boulder. He clutched his knees and watched the surf slide in among rocks, reach for him, and

162

back off again. He wore corduroys and a heavy turtleneck sweater. Dave told him, "It wasn't Kerlee."

He looked up. Distance was in his eyes. It took him a minute to remember where he was. "I always think," he said, "that when I'm in Sangre de Cristo next, I'll stop into a bookstore and buy an atlas. I'll look at a map of the world and put my finger on this spot and run it straight out along whichever parallel it is and know what I'm looking at and not seeing."

"It's the thirty-fifth," Dave said. "You're looking at Yokohama. Ben Orton was seen dead by two witnesses before that tote bag appeared."

Nowell tossed a pebble into the surf. "Do the police know that?"

"Not here," Dave said. "Not yet. I wanted to talk to you first. One of those witnesses also saw you."

"She must be out of her mind with lust," Nowell said. "You're beautiful—but worth risking a life sentence for?"

"She's boxed in," Dave said, "or thinks she is. Someone else saw her. And not just at the foot of Orton's road. Coming out of his study."

Nowell smiled his tight little smile. "I like the inevitability of it. A woman—of course. It had to be."

Dave shook his head. "Her motive is feeble. Sentimentality—what takes the place of real feelings when there aren't any."

"Sentimentality? Our Daisy? Over whom?"

Dave told him about Suchak. "It called for more than a gesture but that was all she had to give it. Which brings us to the other reason she's not a suspect. It wasn't any gasoline can that smashed in Ben Orton's skull."

"It was a flowerpot," Nowell said. "And that means only one person—Cliff Kerlee."

163

"What they found in Orton's brain were fragments of terra-cotta," Dave said, "but those roof tiles stacked on your terrace are also terra-cotta."

Nowell got to his feet. He did it slowly, stiff and middle-aged. "You shouldn't have come here alone," he said. And lunged. Dave stepped aside, stuck out a foot, Nowell sprawled on the sand. He scrambled up, tensed in a crouch, and stopped moving. Because Cecil had come out of the rocks. He stood watching, blank faced, the shiny shoes in his hand. Nowell sighed, relaxed, and began brushing sand off the corduroys and sweater. "And you didn't," he said.

"Mr. Nowell," Cecil said. "Hi."

"You're Daisy's minion," Nowell said.

"Used to be." Cecil rubbed dust off the shoes with a hand and set them carefully side by side on a tall rock. He sat down on the sand, pulled off his socks, and turned up the wide cuffs of the yellow pants. "Way back yesterday."

"Way back yesterday," Dave told Nowell, "I'd have said you didn't go to Ben Orton's to kill him. You went to negotiate. With Kerlee's petitions as a bargaining tool. Orton could have them if he'd give you points."

"I thought they'd start a nice blaze," Nowell said, "in his fireplace."

"And while it burned, you could sit down like gentlemen and resume the discussion you'd begun that night at your house over brandy and cigars."

"Calmly and"—Nowell eyed Cecil, who eased a long foot into the surf—"in private." He looked at Dave again. "You were right, yesterday."

"I guess not. Yesterday I also thought Lester Green killed him. Probably with a brick—there are bricks lying around loose across from his mother's house. He didn't use a brick. He didn't use anything."

164

"Who is Lester Green?" Nowell asked.

Dave told him. He finished, "It would have been an answer for my company. Not the neatest one. That would have been if Louise Orton had killed him." Cecil was up to his ankles in the moving water now, and he bent to roll the pant legs higher. Dave said, "That woman you saw at Nirvana with him that night—she did own an art gallery. Mona Windrow. And one day, Louise Orton marched in there with a gun and told Orton she'd kill him if he didn't stay away from 'that woman.' His answer was to move the woman and the gallery both right into the middle of La Caleta."

"Louise was at home that afternoon," Nowell said. "That was why I went in through the patio. I saw her car in the garage. So why bother me? I didn't get his life-insurance money. I'm not the answer for your company."

"She wasn't strong enough to bash his head in," Dave said. "You are and you did. It wasn't the petitions you wanted from Kerlee's truck, it was the bag. You didn't want to kill Ben Orton. You simply wanted Kerlee convicted for it. And you bet he would be, right after he told the world on television he was going to do it."

"It's warm," Cecil called. He waded out of the surf, stripped and tossed away the yellow jacket, pulled the jersey over his head, kicked out of the yellow pants. Little white knit shorts divided his darkness. He ran back into the surf, splashes arching away from him, glossy with sunset reds. Beyond the tide rocks, he fell forward. His dark head bobbed, his long and shiny arms stretched, disappeared, stretched again. He laughed. "It's warm," he shouted.

"You saw the chance of a lifetime and jumped at it," Dave told Nowell. "Up in the state assembly that time, Kerlee turned twenty-five years of your work and hope to

165

nothing. It was irresistible. If I could admire murder, I'd admire your presence of mind, remembering to drag along that roof tile."

"Save your admiration," Nowell said. "You forget that when Daisy Flynn saw me on the road past the cannery, I was only on my way up there and he was already dead."

"Maybe it happened another way," Dave said. "You went to talk, he got nasty, pulled a gun, and you killed him. Then you went to get Kerlee's bag. He had a gun in his hand."

"What?" Nowell's face twisted in disbelief. "Who says so? All right, I dropped that tote bag beside the body. Is that a crime? I don't think so. I don't know. But one thing I do know. There was no gun in Ben Orton's hand."

The house had its back to the sun this time but the curtains were still drawn at the windows in the wide arches. The garage was empty. There wasn't enough breeze up here to move the leaves of the lacy eucalyptus trees. There was no sound from the shifting water of the blue bay below. A bird cried across the sundown hills—*killdee, killdee!* Dave pushed the wrought-iron patio gate. Daisy Flynn had been right—the hinges squeaked. The cold leaves of the big tropical plants flapped at him as he went among them, shucking his jacket. He handed it to Cecil and stood at the mossy tile fountain, rolling up the sleeves of his shirt. He bent and slid his arms into the murky green water where shadow fish arrowed away out of sight. He groped in the coldness. It was deeper than he'd hoped. He took off the shirt and handed it to Cecil.

"What part of the alphabet is this?" Cecil said.

"A," Dave said. "This is where I should have begun." He plunged his arms in again, this time to the shoulder, turning his face aside. And it was there, lumpy and slick. His fingers tried for grips and found broken edges. He pulled a chunk out of the water and set it on the flat tile edge of the pool. Water ran off it and out of it and puddled around his shoes. "I hadn't been in La Caleta an hour yesterday morning when Jerry Orton told me the patio had water splashed around in it when he got here after his father's death. I couldn't have come back then—he wouldn't have let me. But I ought to have come back a whole hell of a lot sooner than this."

"Yeah, Daisy mentioned it was wet," Cecil said.

"So did Lester." Dave bent again and felt around deep in the water, brought up a second dripping chunk and fitted its broken edges to the broken edges of the first. "But that was too late to save old Tyree Smith. If I'd understood Jerry when he told me about the splashes, I could have closed this case right then." He shook his hands and tried to paw the water off his arms.

"Smith? The old dude that drowned himself?"

Dave reached for his shirt. "He was pushed," he said. "Probably knocked on the head with his own vodka bottle and then pushed." He put the shirt on and buttoned it.

"This is some old Mexican sculpture," Cecil said. "What's the connection?"

"I don't like to be the one to tell you," Dave said. "Because you'll blame yourself."

"Me?" Cecil stared. "What are you talking about? I don't even know what this thing is."

Dave eyed the stout clay figure with its spiked helmet and dwarfish legs. "It's not what it is that counts," he said. "It's what it isn't." He tucked the shirttails into his waistband. "It isn't a flowerpot."

"This is what smashed Orton's head in?" Cecil whistled

softly, flapped Dave's jacket over his shoulder, and put both hands under the figure. He lifted it a little, the broken edges grating. "Heavy. Whoever did it would have to be strong." He set it down carefully and winced at Dave against the dying light. "I don't want it to be somebody else who tells me. I want it to be you. Why would I blame myself?"

"Because you put me on television," Dave said. "That was how the man who ditched this thing learned who I was. Smith had been—what?—an associate of his. Underfoot. A nuisance. He was trying to get him to go away, back up the coast where he came from. I think he'd given him money for the purpose but Smith used it to get drunk instead. Smith ended up talking to me in a bar, and the man saw us together, but he didn't add it up to danger until he learned from the late news who I was and why I was in La Caleta. Then Smith became a menace."

"When Smith called you at the motel," Cecil said, "what did he say? Why did you really go out to his trailer?"

"He said he could tell me who killed Ben Orton," Dave said. "I didn't think so. I thought he was just frightened of being alone. Like I told Jerry Orton. He wanted company."

"Whoever killed him thought he knew," Cecil said.

"It looks that way." Dave sighed, pulled the jacket off Cecil's shoulder and flapped into it. "Think you're strong enough to carry half of this?"

Cecil picked it up. "What can a person do to earn a living that doesn't hurt anybody?"

"I'm a sententious jerk." Dave carried the other half of the figure out through the shrill gate. "I was told that only this morning."

"Then how about a sententious answer," Cecil said.

"All right. Look out for that word *earn.*" Dave hinged forward the flimsy bucket seat on the passenger side of the rental car and set the two halves of the broken figure to-gether on the tough new carpet behind the seat. "What it probably means is *take.*" He clicked the seat back into place and untangled an arm from a hanging safety strap. "In the kinds of jobs you'd want, that's what it's likely to mean."

"And you," Cecil said.

"And I," Dave said. "So what we do is to give, every chance we have—right? Get in."

The figure thudded hard against the back of Cecil's seat when Dave stopped the car suddenly at the gates in the weathered chainlink fence around the grounds of the can-nery. Beyond the weedy stretch of abandoned sand, the clumsy old building lurching out into the surf, the sun laid a fiery sheen on the waves. Sandpipers, busy with their needle beaks, cast long, spindly shadows. A dozen gulls hunched at rest on the rusty cannery roof. Dave left the motor idling and got out of the car. The sun had flicked a bright reflection at him. It had come off the padlock. He lifted the lock and dropped it on its chain. When Cecil came up behind him, he said:

"This is something else I didn't understand yesterday. Didn't understand and should have questioned, and didn't."

Cecil fingered the lock. He looked along the sagging fence. He looked at Dave. "New," he said. "And the gate's old. Everything here is old." He gripped the wire mesh, put his face close to it, like a kid shut out of a playground. He gazed down the broken blacktop road to the cannery load-ing bay. "Nobody's used this place in years."

"That's what I thought. Wrong." Dave crouched. Small

169

purple-blue stains were on the gritty earth. He picked up a half-crushed blossom, stood, and held it out to Cecil.

"Jacaranda?" Cecil said.

"Off the shoes of the man"—Dave let the blossom fall—"who stood here to work this padlock. So he could use this place."

"What for?" Cecil asked. "What man?"

"The one who dumped that figure in the fountain. I don't want to tell you his name till I'm sure. The artsy-craftsy lady he sleeps with owns a gallery full of those figures. And right outside the gallery door is a jacaranda tree." Dave tugged thoughtfully at the padlock. It was expensive, strong, and its insides would be complicated. He let it go, stepped back, and judged the fence. "As to what for—that's what I need to know next."

"Mona Windrow?" Cecil asked. "But Daisy said Ben Orton was sleeping with her."

"And three's a crowd," Dave said. "Give me a boost." Cecil made a stirrup of his hands, then squatted enough so Dave could set a foot in them. Dave stretched, fastened fingers in the fence, and said, "Now—straighten up." Cecil straightened. His hat fell off. Dave lodged the toes of the canvas shoes in the mesh and carefully tugged at the barb-wire that topped the fence. It was limp with age and powdery with rust. He shifted to where he could reach one of the angled struts that held the strands. He crimped and twisted the lowest strand against the strut. It broke. So did the middle strand. He let them dangle and eased over the fence, keeping flat so as to miss the top strand. He dropped inside the fence. "Thanks," he said. "You want to find Jerry Orton for me, please? Right away? Start at city hall. Show him that figure. Tell him where we found it. And bring him back here. On the double. Okay?"

"Okay." Cecil picked up his hat. The slanting sun put the crosswork pattern of the fence on his puzzled face. "Only how is this supposed to get your company's money back?"

Dave shrugged. "I must be working. Somebody's about to get hurt."

"Yeah." Cecil ran the plume between his fingers and put the hat back on. "Will fingerprints still be on that thing? After all that time in the water?"

"Yes, if it matters," Dave said. "They'll be greasy. He runs a boat and he's his own mechanic. And it happened right after he docked."

18

Signs had been tacked to the cannery, but a long time ago, and the red brushwork of the warnings had almost faded out. DANGER. CONDEMNED. UNSAFE. KEEP OUT. He climbed warped steps to the truck loading dock. Shoreside, away from the brunt of the weather, it still felt sturdy underfoot. But its barnlike sliding door didn't budge when he heaved at it. The overhead rollers looked rusted to their tracks. He chose the deck to the left, the one where gaps in the planks had been repaired with bright new boards. It led all the way out to the end of the long, sad building. The railing wasn't in shape. In places it had fallen away. He leaned gingerly on it to look at the dark water below, curling and foaming around weed-hung, barnacled pilings.

He found a door. Boarded up. He went on for another twenty yards and there was a second door like the first. He tugged at one of the boards. The nailheads popped and the board came away in his hands. He swung and tossed it over

172

the railing into the tide. The nails in the second board came away as easily. He drew back, careful where he stood, and gave the door a kick. It fell in with a rip of hinge screws in rotten wood. Dust billowed up. The door tilted and slid through a yawn in the floor and splashed below.

Gripping the doorframe, he leaned inside. The place looked vastly empty but the light was poor. Decades of salt spray had blinded the high windows. The only real light struck down through cankered holes in the roof past big, white wooden crossbeams held by bolts that had been bleeding rust for a long time. Among the wooden beams and the beams of light, swallows flickered in and out of lumpy mud nests. The twittering of the birds echoed shrill in the emptiness. Dave edged a foot around the doorframe and tried a floorboard. It felt secure. Keeping a grip on the doorframe, he put his weight on the board. It held and he let go the doorframe and was standing inside the building in the gloom, the piercing cries of the swallows above, the hiss and wash of the sea below.

He wished for the flashlight that was in the Electra, sunk on its flat tires under the Bayfront Motel. He groped his way through the dark, testing each board as he went and holding to wall studs. Something hulked up between him and the frail light. Not all of the machinery was gone. Here were banks of pipe, plate steel, gears, cogwheels, broken and drooping conveyor belts. The pale faces of gauges peered at him. He seemed to smell the reek of cooking fish again. He went a good many steps before the machinery was not beside him anymore. And it was very dark. The sea had muscle out here and the old structure shook. He began not to trust the flooring. Maybe he had guessed wrong, maybe he ought to give this up.

Then he thought the structure was shaking because

something was hitting it, something solid. *Clunk* it went in the darkness. *Clunk. Clunk.* Measured, hollow, heavy. And each time, the floor shivered. He smiled grimly to himself. He saw Tyree Smith again, drunk, unsteady on his legs, under the jacaranda tree. *Where do you keep that boat of yours?* Voices, sea-washed, wind-tattered, talked about fog and tides and hauls of fish through the shiny radio on the shelf in back of Ben Orton's desk. Dave pushed away from the half safety of the cannery wall. It was down there in the dark. Not far now, not far.

He let the muffled thudding guide him. And a tall slit of light so narrow it kept flickering out. Where doors met? He took maybe twenty steps on flooring without flaw. Then he stepped out on nothing. The surprise made him cry out. The sound went up to the metal roof and ricocheted off it, and for an instant the swallows were silent. Falls in the dark were all alike—you couldn't judge how long they took. He expected water. It wasn't water. He hit an ungiving horizontal surface—on his feet but off balance.

Then he struck his head.

Something prodded him roughly in the gut. He groaned and rolled away from it. It prodded him in the left kidney. He wanted to escape it and he tried to crawl. Pain burst inside his skull. He lay still. The pain slowly dulled. He touched his head and his hand came away wet and sticky. The prod was to his ribs this time and less prod than kick. He rolled over again, careful of his head now, but not able to be careful enough. The pain made him yelp. He waited for it to back off, then opened his eyes. Light slammed into them, the fierce dying light of the sky. He shut his eyes. But his other senses worked. The planks he lay on vibrated. There was the beat of an engine beneath them, the quaver of a propeller shaft. He heard water slicing off a bow, the tumble of water at a far stern. The deck lifted under him and dropped. Vomit rose in his throat. Not from the motion—he didn't get seasick. It had to be from concussion. He couldn't focus right but the hand he showed himself was thick with blood from his head. He panted quickly, shallowly against the nausea. He was gripped roughly under the arms. Al Franklin's face, bearded, sunburned, was upside down above him. He hauled Dave to his feet.

"Come on, you prying son of a bitch. Off my boat and out of my goddam life." He swung Dave around in a bear hug. Red horizon, the white superstructure of the boat, a dazzle of glass wheeled sickly. Dave sagged. Franklin staggered. "Help yourself, for Christ's sake. This wreck won't steer itself. I haven't got time to fuck around with you." The boat pitched. Spray flew up. They did a drunken waltz. The boat yawed. They came hard and together against a wooden gunwale. Franklin gripped him around the middle and tried to lift him. Very far off, Dave glimpsed shoreline, tiny La Caleta with sundown sparking off its windows. The boat plowed into a wave and shuddered. White water foamed around their legs. The scuppers sucked. Franklin staggered off balance again. Dave gripped the rail, raised himself—the pain ripping around inside his skull—and brought a foot down hard on Franklin's instep. It was protected only by a sandal. Franklin let him go, so suddenly Dave dropped to his knees. He skidded on his knees across the wet deck and slammed up against the edge of an open hatch. Below were broken crates and bundles of packing straw. Franklin fell on Dave's back, wrenching at him. Dave sank teeth into his fingers. Franklin clubbed him with a fist above the ear. Dave blacked out. He woke facedown in his own vomit. He turned. Franklin stood over him, long hair flying. The ship tilted and he sat down hard on the deck. Something was under Dave's hand, a shaft of cold, wet metal. Franklin lurched to his feet and flung himself at Dave. Dave swung the crowbar at Franklin's head. It connected. Franklin rolled with the ship and came to rest crumpled against the gunwale.

Dave dragged himself toward the wheelhouse.

"The fountain didn't soak all the blood and hair off," Jerry Orton said. "I could see it. And his greasy prints. I didn't need the lab. Or you. I needed an arrest."

"All of a sudden," Dave said wryly. He lay in a long, new room where high beds were shut off from each other by white canvas sheets laced inside pipe frames on wheels. He had the best bed, the one next to the window since the ward was empty. The private rooms of La Caleta's little one-story hospital were filled. One of them with Al Franklin. Through the window, Dave could see the blue bay, the ragged black rocks, the floating brown kelp. A pair of otters played among the kelp. While he'd pushed a bland breakfast around with his fork, he'd watched an otter lie on its back in the water, clutch a leg-waving crab against its chest, rip it apart, and stuff the meat into its mouth. It looked as if it were chortling. "So you went to the gallery and asked for him in a loud voice and let Mona Windrow keep you talking while he beat it out the back door and down to his boat." Dave coughed a short, hurtful laugh. "Maybe you didn't need me. I sure as hell needed you."

"Never." Jerry Orton shook his neat head. "You handled the bastard." He sounded disgusted at himself. "You handled it all. Just fine."

"Not in the right order," Dave said.

"I got in your way," Orton said. "I apologize."

Dave shrugged. And winced. His muscles ached. "You were trying to protect your family. So tell me—what does Franklin say? Why did he kill your father?"

"Self-defense. My father was going to turn him in. When Franklin walked through the patio doors, carrying one of those things—to show him the trip had been, well, a success —my father was waiting for him with a gun."

"What kind of success?" Dave wondered.

"Hell, he'd got what he went after. My father financed the trip. It was Mona Windrow's idea. Franklin's her brother. He knows Mexico, Yucatan, Guatemala. She told us this morning. All about those old idols, or whatever you call them."

"An archaeologist?" Dave said.

"He worked for them—museums, universities. Managed the expeditions, the practical side, supplies, ships, jeeps, trucks, all that. He must have known the right places to dig. He brought back a whole shipload, didn't he?"

"So why did your father meet him with a gun?"

"Because he'd found out it was illegal. Those things are national treasures, even the ones still buried in the jungle. The Mexican government practically kills you for taking them out of the country, and the U.S. cooperates. It's kind of ironic—something my father read in that book on Mexican art Mona Windrow gave him tipped him off. And he wrote to the experts at the L.A. County Museum. I found the letter they sent him in his den last night. That's how I know for sure." His eyes were blue, clear, and innocent. He stood like a staunch Cub Scout. "But I told you before. My father would never get mixed up in anything illegal."

"You told me." Dave nodded and shut his eyes. He was getting double vision again, and the pain in his head was coming back. "I didn't believe you then. He framed Lester

Green on a marijuana charge. He burned down Eddie Suchak's paper when it was going to print the reason why. He had a pretty specialized view of what was legal and not." Dave opened his eyes. "I still don't believe you. What does Franklin say—was that the explanation your father gave him?"

"All Franklin says is what happened, not what anybody said or why." Orton's face was red. "Why would you believe him and not me? A smuggler. A murderer."

"Because you accepted everything your father ever told you," Dave said. "You never questioned him in your life. You're a true believer. They make bad witnesses."

"You don't understand," Orton said. "There are times the law is too slow. It's not flexible. There are wrong things that get done that aren't in the statute books. You have to deal with them when you're a law-enforcement officer. You can't let them go on."

"Like your sister marrying Lester Green?"

"That was a personal thing, a private, family matter," Orton said. "This was a government thing. My father was a loyal American."

"Explain one thing to me." Dave heard the fragile jingling of a trolley and looked toward the open door at the end of the long aisle between the sterile, empty beds. "If your father didn't know what he was putting his money into was illegal, why did he fix up the cannery as a place to dock and unload the boat in secret?"

Orton flushed. "So my mother wouldn't know. About him and Mona Windrow. If they unloaded at the bayfront and carted the stuff to the gallery in broad daylight right in front of God and everybody, people would ask questions, they'd make the connection, they'd gossip and she'd hear about it. And she was jealous. It was only a business ar-

178

rangement, but she wouldn't see it that way. I don't know why. She didn't have any reason. He wasn't that kind of man. They had a perfect marriage."

The pain in Dave's head got worse. He had to close one eye to see Orton right. The nausea was coming back. He said, "Ask your wife what kind of man he was."

"No." Orton shook his head desperately. "Not Dad."

"Tyree Smith had a nice, safe life up there in his little back room at Mona Windrow's gallery in Monterey," Dave said. "Then your father and Franklin broke it up."

"What's Tyree Smith got to do with this?"

"He had some letters." Dave looked prayerfully toward the door again. "From Al Franklin to Mona Windrow. They'd lied to your father. They weren't brother and sister. They were lovers."

"We burned all that junk from his trailer," Orton said. "Made a bonfire right there on the point."

"They weren't in his trailer," Dave said. "You know where they were. That letter from the museum wasn't all you found in your father's files last night."

Orton looked sick. "How did you find out?"

"I didn't. But I need an explanation that adds up. Your father wouldn't blow a smuggling operation that was about to pay off in ten-thousand-dollar bills just for the sake of the Grand Old Flag. Even you can't believe that now. He wasn't that kind of man, Jerry. But he was the kind of man that would try to kill Al Franklin once he'd seen those letters. And he did."

"Why can't you leave anything alone?" Orton shouted. "Why can't you believe in anything?"

"Don't cry," Dave said. "Tell me how Franklin did it." A tall, flat-chested nurse wheeled in the trolley. Dave said,

"Your father wasn't young but he looked in pretty good shape. And he had a gun. How did Franklin kill him?"

"He charged," Orton said sulkily. "My father pulled the trigger. He missed but Franklin fell down as if he'd been hit. My father went and bent over him and Franklin grabbed a broken chunk of the figure and hit him with it."

The nurse showed horsey teeth in a clockwork smile. "I'm sorry, but it's time for this patient to rest now."

Orton picked up his badge-mounted cap. "Anything I can do," he mumbled and walked off.

"Get me a new set of tires," Dave said.

The nurse folded back the sheet. A hypodermic glinted in the sea light. "Can you turn on your side, please?" she said.

Something soft and light landed on the bed. He opened his eyes. A black face blurred above him. He tried to smile. He reached out. His mouth was dry and numb from the pain-killers they'd shot him up with but he made it shape words. "I wondered if you'd ever get here."

"He never did," the blurred face said.

Dave squeezed his eyes shut and opened them again.

The blurred face said, "And he never will. I brought you back the gift you gave him. And I want you to understand me. You keep away from him, from now on. Is that clear? Are you conscious?"

Dave got the man into focus. He wore a neat, new, pale suit, silver-framed goggles, a moderate Afro. Dave said, "I'm as conscious as they let me get in this place."

"This is the fourth college I put him in. To get him away from it. And it worked till you showed up. But you aren't staying. That's what he says. You belong in L.A. And that is fine. You go back to L.A. and let Cecil alone."

180

"He's twenty-one," Dave said.

"Not for eighteen months, and I told our mother when she died that I would look after him, and with the Lord's help I am going to keep my promise, and you are no part of it. If you come near him again, I'll see that you go to jail."

"His brother's keeper," Dave said.

"You got it," the neat man said, "and it is not easy."

"It won't get any easier," Dave said.

"It will, if you go away," the neat man said.

"I will if you will," Dave said, and turned to the window.

When he woke again, it was the flat-chested nurse who stood beside the bed. She blinked at the yellow hat. Dave hadn't touched it. It lay where the neat man had dropped it. She picked it up and turned it in her hands. Brows raised, she looked from the hat to Dave and back at the hat again.

Dave said: "I thought I'd wear it out of here. To hide the bandages."

She shook her head and hung it on the lamp. "It isn't you," she said.